"Jan wondered i

"You can tell her I did, Rowan responded p y turned her back to the man on horseback to continue picking. Her hands trembled just a little as she parted the tall grass to expose the scarlet globes. Rowan became conscious of her thudding heart as the silence lengthened. Had Neal left as silently through the woods as he had come?

She looked over her shoulder as casually as she could and saw that he had dismounted and was lounging in the soft grass. She turned quickly as he looked her way.

"Finding any?"

"A few," she muttered without turning around.

He reclined on the gentle slope, propped up on one elbow as he watched from hooded eyes her hunt for the elusive treats. He was a little surprised at her short responses, but his eyes softened at the petite figure hunched over the berry patch, the graceful movement of her tanned arms a pleasure to watch.

Her size had nothing to do with her ability to work, he had decided. And under the most primitive conditions— the stifling kitchen, the black monster of a cookstove. He sighed and stretched out, pillowing his head on his arms.

Rowan stood up and stretched her cramped legs, wincing at the pain. She started back toward the path with her half-filled bucket of strawberries, intending to walk right by Neal. A gentle snore stopped her in midstep.

"Neal?" He didn't stir and she approached hesitantly. "Neal?" she repeated. She dropped down on her knees beside him. *So the boss is vulnerable after all*, she thought.

This Band of Gold

GEORGIA DALLAS

BOOKS
of the Zondervan Publishing House
Grand Rapids, Michigan

A Note from the Author:
I love to hear from my readers! You may correspond with me by writing:
Georgia Dallas
Author Relations
1415 Lake Drive, S.E.
Grand Rapids, MI 49506

THIS BAND OF GOLD
Copyright © 1987 by Georgia Dallas

Serenade/Serenata is an imprint of Zondervan Publishing House, 1415 Lake Drive, S.E., Grand Rapids, MI 49506.

ISBN 0-310-47321-7

All rights reserved. No part of this publication may be reproduced, stored in a retrieval system, or transmitted in any form or by any means— electronic, mechanical, photocopy, recording, or any other—except for brief quotations in printed reviews, without the prior permission of the publisher.

Edited by Nancye Willis and Anne Severance
Designed by Kim Koning

Printed in the United States of America

87 88 89 90 91 92 / EE / 10 9 8 7 6 5 4 3 2 1

To Jim
You said I could do it!

chapter 1

ROWAN HAYLEY WAS OBLIVIOUS TO THE HEADS that turned and the eyes that followed her petite figure as she hurried through the crowded concourse. Dodging other deplaning travelers, she glanced at her watch and a tolerant little smile tugged at the corners of the full mouth. If Jan were running true to form, she wouldn't be waiting in the baggage claim area, but would arrive a little late, a little breathless, and very apologetic.

She followed the arrows through the corridors, scanning the throng for the tall, dark-haired figure of her friend, then stood well back while her fellow passengers plucked their luggage from the spinning carousel. Only when the crowd cleared did she retrieve her large bag and a smaller overnight case and carry them to a nearby seat.

If Jan didn't find her soon, Rowan would have her paged; in the meantime, it wasn't unpleasant to sit and watch the people stream past. She settled back and played a little game, speculating on where they were going, or where they had been. As she somewhat wistfully watched joyous reunions and reluctant good-bys, a familiar loneliness washed over her, leaving her shaken by its intensity. A lifetime ago, she, too, had had a family of her own.

THIS BAND OF GOLD

Then, nearly three years ago, a truck had roared across the grassy median, crushing the compact car in which Rowan was riding, and with it, all her dreams. The accident had left her widowed and childless, barren even of the new life she had been carrying.

There! That sturdy little boy in the stroller just passing! He looked so like Robbie with his head of curly blond hair and that toothless grin. She looked away abruptly, stung by the memory of her son. He had been the image of Philip. Everybody said so. Well, if she could not recapture that blissful time with her husband and child, she would at least remember them. Unconsciously, she fingered the wide gold band on her left hand.

Rowan took measured breaths until she had regained some semblance of composure. But the sight of that tot had stirred all her misgivings about this trip to Twelve Oaks.

Until now, she had successfully evaded Jan's invitations to visit the resort deep in the Missouri Ozarks jointly owned and operated by Jan and her brother Neal. She preferred instead to leave the delicate balance of her existence undisturbed, allowing not a single crack in the protective façade she managed to maintain. She was satisfied with her career as fashion buyer for one of Chicago's largest department stores, and if the job demanded a frenetic pace, it also produced a kind of mindless, almost hypnotic lifestyle that left little time for such memories as those of the moment.

Even more disturbing than the disruption of her comfortable routine was the fact that her friend Jan was a committed—and vocal—Christian. If she started in on

"God's will" and "finding his plan for your life," Rowan wasn't sure she could handle it.

The soft mouth thinned in a grimace as she looked up to scan the crowd again. Failing to spot Jan, Rowan sighed and settled back. Her eyes fell on the pronounced grain of the cowhide luggage at her feet, her mind whirling. This whole trip was a mistake! Another thought occurred to her.

Jan had written that Neal, too, had been "born again" and was a changed person. Rowan swallowed a mirthless little laugh. The last thing she needed was to come face to face with a pious, preachy Neal. In fact, she didn't care to see Neal, period.

Once he had been a part of her life, light-years ago, when she and Jan had been roommates at the University of Illinois. She shifted restlessly on the hard seat as she thought about Neal and his romantic overtures in those long-ago days. His relentless pursuit had only frightened her and she had fled, confused by the emotions he aroused. What a little fool she had been then, she thought derisively. No longer was she the naïve young Christian who trusted God to protect her from overzealous suitors —and runaway trucks. Bitter reality had taken care of that.

In the intervening years, she had had no contact with Neal. And Jan's occasional references to his activities or whereabouts had stirred no interest on her part. Now she was invading his territory, so to speak, and thoughts of the man nagged persistently. Though Jan had assured her he would be away on a business trip, Rowan could not help feeling uneasy.

Instinct told her to take the next flight back to Chicago. She moved to the edge of her seat, slipped her arm into the shoulder strap of her tan leather bag, and stood purposefully. She would leave a message for Jan ...

"Rowan?"

She froze, then whirled around, her eyes wide in disbelief. "Neal! What are you doing here?" she blurted.

"Jan sends her apologies. She wanted to meet you herself, but she couldn't get away."

He smiled Neal's slow smile and studied her intently with Neal's cool gray gaze, but this Neal was almost unrecognizable. The once dark brown hair liberally sprinkled with gray was now a shock of pure white that framed the deeply tanned craggy features, while a full mustache softened the furrows and planes of his face.

An arresting maturity, intensified by the rugged appearance, was even more compelling than the youthful Neal she had known. Instead of the staid pin-stripe suit and silk shirts he had favored, this sun-bronzed giant wore faded jeans and a blue workshirt open at the neck.

"Please excuse my appearance," he said as if reading her mind. "I didn't have time to change." One heavy eyebrow arched, a quizzical look crossing his face when she made no comment. He waited, a springing tension in his stance belying his calm demeanor.

For the life of her, Rowan couldn't say a word, her customary aplomb deserting her as she stared up at him with shadowed green eyes. His very physical presence was an affront; the earthy virility once camouflaged by conservative business attire was now accentuated by the casual clothes he wore. He was so—so alive, while Philip ... A sickening lurch of her stomach jolted her to action. She bent down to pick up her overnight case.

"I'm sorry. I was just leaving." She avoided his eyes and moved to pick up the larger bag.

"Leaving?" A large brown hand closed over the slender fingers on the handle. "That's what I'm here for—to take you to Twelve Oaks."

"You don't understand." She dared to look up into the brilliant eyes, so close now. "I'm going back to Chicago," she said firmly. "I'll call Jan . . . " She gave a futile yank on the handle of the cowhide bag, the set of her slim shoulders confirming her determination.

He pulled the bag from her grasp easily and set it on the floor. "Here, sit down," he commanded, seating himself.

She glared at him. "I just told you. I'm leaving." Suddenly she felt like stamping her foot to make him listen. "I have to get my ticket changed."

"Just sit down for a moment, will you?" He patted the seat beside him.

His stone-colored eyes traveled slowly from her beige high-healed sandals to the top of her soft toast-brown hair as she stood tensely before him. Reluctantly, she sank slowly onto the narrow seat.

"Now—" he turned toward her—"what am I to tell Jan? That you came this far and decided to return to Chicago without seeing her, rather than ride with her favorite brother?" Amusement twitched at the firm lips beneath the mustache.

The man was impossible! Mutinously, she met his inscrutable gaze, her own eyes jade-green with anger. "Just tell her I'll call her later. She'll understand." She made a move as if to rise.

"Relax, Rowan." He lounged casually against the railing, one arm draped over the back of her seat. "I'm not going to try to change your mind. Neither am I going to argue with you. I just want to talk to you for a moment. Please?" he added softly.

Her belligerence left with a rush, leaving her weak enough to lean back gratefully, a wary eye on him. His unassuming plea surprised her, but this man knew every trick in the book. She wouldn't be taken in by this humility angle.

"That's better," he said. "Now, Rowan, what we had together was a long time ago." He held up a hand at a sound from her. "Let me finish. Jan needs to see you this summer, you obviously need a vacation, and I'll be away most of the time. I suggest we let bygones be bygones and try to be civil when we *are* together." He searched her face, noting the thin cheeks and shadowed eyes. "What do you say?"

She glared at him, simmering at his arrogant arrangement of her schedule. She wanted no part of this "vacation." Still, something about the idea was intriguing, and she allowed herself to savor the prospect. No deadlines, fresh air, a change of pace . . . She drew a deep breath, feeling a release of tension in the taut shoulders.

"Well?"

Mesmerized, she watched the chiseled mouth form the word. The crowds milled about them, a kaleidoscope of sound and color. She shook her head to clear it. What was he saying? Oh, yes, she couldn't let Jan down and, after all, Neal was simply someone she had known long ago.

"You're right, of course," she said decisively, wondering at the same time why she should feel piqued that he had dismissed their earlier relationship so easily. Something else annoyed her, too. "Is it so obvious I'm in need of a vacation?"

He gave a short bark of laughter. "Rowan, you're so uptight you're ready to shatter into a million pieces. A few weeks in the country will do you a world of good." He looked pointedly at her hands clenched in her lap, lingering on the broad gold band on her left hand. "Let go, Rowan," he said softly. "It's all over."

She smothered a tremulous cry as the pink flush of anger tinged her pale cheeks. Blindly, she looked about as she stood, poised for flight. "Who are you to tell . . . ?" She choked on the words that grated between clenched teeth.

"Never mind that now," he said and rose swiftly to pick up her bag with one hand and propel her toward the escalator with the other.

Not a word passed between them as they left the congested highway near the airport. Rowan sat rigidly in her corner, staring straight ahead. Her right hand covered her left as it lay in her lap, her thumb surreptitiously caressing her wedding band.

Family and friends had long since given up suggesting its removal from the slender finger. That Neal had been presumptuous enough to give the same advice infuriated her. She seethed in silence, despair following swiftly as her anger ebbed.

THIS BAND OF GOLD

No one seemed to understand that the heavy gold ring was a tangible link with Philip, representing a love as enduring as the precious metal from which it was fashioned. It was a talisman, a charm, against any foolish act or commitment on her part, strengthening any weakness that might tempt her to replace the one love of her life. It had become a touchstone, a rock of remembrance, by which all others were judged.

There could be only one Philip, only one Robbie. She wanted no replacements or substitutions. As long as the shining band encircled her finger, she was safe from any involvement. Philip had worn its twin to his grave, and so would she.

Rowan cast a sidelong glance at Neal. He was intent on his driving. She was foolish to let him rile her. His opinions were of no concern to her. He knew nothing of the woman she had become, of the life she had lived, so how could he possibly know what was best for her? Still, she would keep her promise to his sister and pay a token visit before returning to Chicago.

She gloated smugly to herself. Soon she would be in the sanctuary of her small apartment. There, she could keep the world at bay and relegate Neal Conrad to the past where he belonged. She could enjoy the rest of her vacation at her own pace, reading until the wee hours of the morning if she so desired, a luxury she denied herself in the usual work week. Perhaps she wouldn't even let anyone know she was back. A secret little smile tugged at her lips as she rotated the golden circle that symbolized her world.

She stole another glance at Neal's profile. He was ignoring her, but the slight flexing of his jaw betrayed his awareness of her presence beside him. Could it be that he had been as nervous as she about their meeting after all these years? If that were the case, he had carried it off very well, daring to tread on delicate ground and getting her defenses up from the first moment.

She willed herself to relax, her head against the headrest, eyes closed against the glare of the late afternoon sun. The hum of the heavy car was soothing, lulling her into a boneless lethargy that was unusual for her. Her eyelids were too heavy to lift more than a little. A shimmering haze danced under the partly closed lids. It was pleasantly cool, and the dark fan of lashes fluttered down once more as she gave up the struggle.

Neal's craggy features assumed a softness Rowan would have been surprised to see if she had been able to keep her eyes open. She was too pale, he mused, the green eyes too large in the white face. Too thin, too, although she wore the expensive designer clothes well. His discerning ear had detected the emptiness in her voice, and a sensitivity born of his new faith moved him to a wrenching pity for her. Better not let the pity show. It would only drive her away. Again. He couldn't live with that.

He had blundered once, years ago. She had been so young and beguilingly innocent then. And he, over-confident and brash, had pursued her relentlessly with characteristic single-mindedness. Instead, his plan had backfired and sent her fleeing. Well, he couldn't say he didn't believe in miracles. She had come into his life again—and this time he wouldn't let her get away.

He knew from conversations with Jan that Rowan liked her job as a fashion buyer and was good at it. He guessed that the fast-paced position allowed little time for close friendships. It figured. In her present frame of mind, she wouldn't be looking for that kind of complication.

What he hadn't reckoned on was her stubborn refusal to acknowledge that death had terminated her marriage vows. That wedding ring on her finger had given him quite a start.

Somehow, he had to make her realize that though her husband and child were gone, she had her whole life to live—preferably with him. Even if she refused him, he wanted to see the shadows leave the sea-green eyes and hear laughter bubble from the full lips again.

What hurt even more was knowing that she had turned her back on God. He knew she was a Christian; in fact, her faith had been one of the things that had attracted him to her when he himself had been seeking something real and solid. But now she couldn't see beyond her own pain.

He glanced at her again. She looked so defenseless. His knuckles whitened on the steering wheel. Her stoic acceptance that her life was over was intolerable—wrong. He caught the flicker of an eyelid and busied himself with his driving.

She stirred and stretched. He smiled to himself. *Bet she'd much rather be waking up back in Chicago.*

"It won't be long now," he announced.

She heard the quiet voice beside her, and her heart thudded in panic as memory returned. She really was in the car with Neal! She risked a glance from half-closed lids and groaned inwardly. The denim-clad thighs and booted feet in her line of vision were all too real.

In one motion, she sat up and opened her eyes, all senses alert. The lethargy was gone, the resolve to leave as soon as possible foremost in her mind.

"Maybe Jan will have time to show you the sights while you're here."

"That would be nice," she lied coolly. "The sights" nor anything else here interested her that much.

Abruptly, Neal veered the car off the road and pulled into a wide parking area designated as a lookout point and protected by a low stone wall.

Rowan was annoyed and puzzled. Why stop now when they were almost to the resort? The sooner they got there, the sooner she could leave.

"I thought the tour started later."

Without a word, he got out and came around to open her door. "Just humor me."

She thought of simply refusing; then the silver eyes held hers for an instant. Reluctantly she stepped out.

She dallied, removing her jacket and arranging it neatly over the back of the seat while he strode to the stone barrier.

He chuckled to himself when he realized she was stalling, avoiding him. At least there was still a healthy spark of *something*.

She sauntered to the wall, finally perching some distance from him. She watched him standing quietly with his shoulders hunched, hands braced on the wall, a faraway look in his eyes. She turned her head to follow his gaze.

He let the silence lengthen before he spoke. "You're in the Ozark highlands now," he said quietly. "The hills aren't as high here in southern Missouri as farther south in Arkansas, where they meet the Ouachitas, but they're still high enough and rocky enough to limit road building to some degree and guarantee some isolation. The unspoiled 'wilderness' feeling is what lures the tourists who want to get away from it all." He glanced her way. "They seem to like Twelve Oaks for that reason."

Who cares? she thought. The sun was hot and she wanted to leave.

In spite of herself, though, her eyes strayed to the distant hills, the variegated greens of the undulating tree-capped elevations stretching as far as the eye could see. Dollhouse homesteads nestled in the folds, guarding black specks of cattle pastured on the steep hillsides. The hills cupped mysterious purple-shadowed hollows and valleys, intersected by the curving ribbon of highway that wound into infinity. Even the intermittent eruptions of limestone outcroppings were singularly beautiful. Above them, dollops of whipped-cream clouds garnished an azure sky.

"Over there," he lifted a bronzed arm, "is the Huzzah River. It flows right through Twelve Oaks property. The water is still relatively clean, and the fishing is good. We won't be able to see it until we get to the resort, though."

She caught the caressing cadence and deepening timbre of his voice as he spoke of his beloved hills, a curious warmth coursing through her veins that had nothing to do with the hot sun well past its zenith. As he continued to extol the beauty of the hills and river, she turned away from his keen gaze and pretended to study the scenery.

"Like it?"

How could anyone with eyes not like it? It was enchanting. She shrugged. "It's all right, I guess, if you like trees."

His lips tightened, but he made no comment as she rose. "May we go on now?"

"Not just yet." He raised one booted foot to the wall and leaned his elbow on his knee. "First, I want to apologize."

"Apologize? For what?"

"For my gratuitous advice back in the airport." His eyes swept her left hand where it rested on the strap of her shoulder bag.

She resisted the urge to whip her hand behind her back, and forced herself to incline her head in a gesture of acceptance. "That's quite all right," she said distantly, but her heart had set up a disturbed fluttering. She didn't want his apologies, or his sympathy either. She headed for the car.

"Rowan?"

His somber tone halted her in midstride, and she looked back at him.

"Yes?"

"Please believe me when I say I'm deeply sorry for . . . your . . . loss. I'll spare you the platitudes about 'God's will' and 'time healing' and so forth. There's no way I can understand the hell you've gone through . . . that you're still going through," he amended. "But I *am* sorry."

She was touched by his obvious sincerity. She was so weary of soppy sympathy and pretensions of understanding. She lifted her eyes to his. "Thank you," she said simply.

"But I'm sure these hills can help you come to terms with yourself. The hills," he chuckled, "and Jan. She's still the most down-to-earth person I know. By the way, you'd better be prepared. She still believes hard work is the remedy for most anything." He grinned down at her. "Remember the mop episode?"

"How could I forget!" Rowan groaned in mock dismay as she pictured Jan mopping and waxing the entire hall and stairway in their apartment building the night before mid-terms to ease her anxiety over a chemistry exam. "I spent the better part of *that* night rubbing her with Ben-Gay so she could climb the steps to the lab the next morning."

"Well, what are friends for?" He laughed.

Rowan had to smile. He knew his sister well.

"One more thing . . . " He straightened up and moved close, towering over her. "I hate to see you so bitter." He reached out a calloused finger and gently traced the faint line between her brows.

She stiffened at his touch, then widened her eyes in feigned surprise. "Bitter?" she said with mocking innocence. She shook herself free of his touch. "Of course I'm bitter. Who wouldn't be?" She nurtured her bitterness because it helped fuel the anger. And that small, hot coal of anger in the middle of her being told her she was alive. Not living, but alive.

"I lost everything I loved," she said, looking directly into the saddened eyes above her.

"Everything?"

She caught the innuendo in his tone. "*Everything*," she said with finality, and moved swiftly past him to the car.

Before he closed her door, he leaned inside. "A fair warning, Rowan. I always finish what I start—" He straightened up to close the door, and she almost missed his last muttered words "—even if I started it six years ago."

chapter

2

"TWELVE OAKS!"

She roused from her corner as Neal maneuvered the car between simple stone pillars. Massive ancient oaks, six on each side, defined the curving drive. Black scabrous trunks supported the intertwining limbs that created a cool, dim tunnel, leading the eye to the lodge at the far end.

This was anything but the small rustic cabin Rowan had envisioned from Jan's description. Instead, she saw a sprawling structure of vertical cedar siding that hugged the terrain. Blending into the surroundings, it was anchored to the earth by the informal landscaping of sun-bleached boulders. Her eyes followed the steep pitched roof to the row of clerestory windows breaking the roof line.

She turned to Neal with raised eyebrows. "I had no idea."

He smiled. "We wanted to keep the sense of wilderness intact, something rustic but not too primitive; contemporary, but not stark." He couldn't hide the pride in his voice.

"You've certainly achieved that," she said grudgingly. She was no authority, but her aesthetic sense told her the lodge was an outstanding example of the melding of architecture, function, and setting. *And way out here in the middle of nowhere!* she thought in amazement.

"You'll like the inside," he promised. "We've used some old family things and a great many antiques and collectibles from the local . . ." He broke off as the front door opened and a tall young woman flew across the lawn toward them with a joyful squeal.

"Row! I thought you would never get here!"

Rowan found herself enveloped in a bear hug. Then Jan backed off and held her by the shoulders, merry brown eyes greedily assessing her from head to toe, taking in the subdued elegance of the beige linen suit and creamy silk blouse. "You look super, Row, as usual—a regular fashion plate—but you're too pale and thin. Oh, well," she hurried on, "it's nothing that fresh air and sunshine won't cure." With a nod in Neal's direction as he unloaded the luggage, she leaned toward Rowan and said *sotto voce,* "I'm so sorry I couldn't get away to meet you. Everything broke loose at the last minute."

"It really is okay, Jan. Everything turned out just fine," Rowan assured her, then changed the subject before her friend could fire any questions at her. "By the way, I'm impressed." She swept the air with a gesture that encompassed house and grounds. The lawn they were crossing was shaded with century-old oaks, their distinctive five-lobed leaves hanging limp and still in the afternoon heat. "But it isn't exactly what I expected when you wrote about a renovated farmhouse on a few acres of land."

"Well, it really *was* a farmhouse, with a little added here and there. The clerestory windows, for one thing . . . and the dining room we built to connect the old summer kitchen to the house . . . a few balconies . . . a pool." Jan grinned impishly.

"As I said—hardly a typical old farmhouse. And the setting! Everything looks so wonderfully natural."

Jan echoed Neal's words. "We tried to keep it that way. We even used the weathered wood from an old barn for some of the paneling."

"We?"

"Uh-huh. Neal and I." She looked at Rowan with shining eyes. "I think we've both found ourselves here, Row. It's been hard work, but the dividends have been much greater than we ever imagined." She raised her eyes to the backdrop of encircling hills. "Serenity, peace, a sense of God's presence . . ." Seeing the pained look that crossed her friend's face, she broke off with a little laugh. "But don't get me started. You'll see." Then she turned serious again, "We love you, Row. All we want is your happiness."

Rowan's throat tightened, and a small dart of angry envy pierced her heart. Never again would she experience happiness. She knew *Jan* loved her, but she also knew only too well that the complacent existence her friend described could shatter in an instant. "I hope you're right, Jan."

"I know I'm right!" Impulsively, she hugged the other girl. "Rowan Hayley, I can't believe you're really here! But I do hope you brought along something less . . . less sophisticated." She wrinkled her nose appealingly.

Rowan burst out laughing. "Me? Sophisticated? Now I know you've been back in the hills too long, Jan. These are just my working clothes to fool my boss into thinking I'm a knowledgeable, cosmopolitan buyer." She raised her eyebrows and looked haughtily down her pert nose before grinning mischievously. "I didn't think you'd fall for it, too."

Jan cocked her head and eyed Rowan critically. "Well, just look at you. Designer suit, *real* leather bag . . ."

"Please, Jan," Rowan begged, embarrassment staining her cheeks with a becoming flush. "Show me to my room immediately and let me put on my jeans."

"And look like me?" Jan gestured deprecatingly at the faded jeans and sneakers she wore. "Still, I guess this is a more practical costume," she said with a wide grin as she led the way to the lodge.

Same old Jan, Rowan mused as she followed her up the curved walkway. *She still bubbles like a bottle of pop.* Yet, beneath the familiar effervescence, Rowan had glimpsed a new dimension in her old friend, something that had been missing two years ago, when she had seen her last. Curious . . .

Her thoughts stopped short at the front door, replete with brass pineapple doorknocker in the tradition of southern hospitality. And when Jan swung it open, Rowan stepped inside, her quick intake of breath signaling her appreciation.

Her first impression was of massive beams, richly paneled walls, and wide floor boards polished to a satiny finish. Antique chests and small tables, rich with the patina of age, reposed next to deep chairs, arranged to allow an unobstructed view of the mountains through a wall of windows. Handmade baskets of lush greenery hung from the beams, and several potted Norfolk pines filled the corners, seeming to bring the tree-covered slopes right into the room.

"Someone has a great touch," Rowan said admiringly, remembering Jan's description of the derelict property they had purchased. "I particularly like the paneling, Jan. It's so rich and warm."

"Well, we've worked hard," Jan acknowledged and looked around with a pleased smile. "As for the paneling, that was Neal's pet project, and you know what a stickler for detail he is. Would you believe he selected each panel personally, polished it by hand, and matched the grain as each section went up? It took him *months!*

She could well believe that! Neal, fifteen years older, confidant and mentor after the early deaths of their parents. Cool, urbane, worldly Neal. He had visited them at college as often as his travel commitments in his plant management job had allowed. He had always wanted everything to be perfect for his baby sister. Jan was the one person he truly cared about; he had taken his guardianship seriously—so seriously that at times he had nearly driven her wild with his hovering over the details of her life, including where she bought her clothes and whom she dated. Still, Jan never seemed to doubt he wanted only the best for her, and they had always worked out their conflicts amiably.

"I'll show you to your room and you can relax for a while," Jan broke in on her thoughts. "We use the rooms upstairs." She indicated the broad steps at the far end of the room. "The cottages in back are for paying guests."

Rowan followed her up the stairs to a room at the back of the house, where she found her luggage waiting outside the door.

"Rowan, I'm really sorry I couldn't meet your plane," Jan apologized again as she helped carry the luggage into the room.

"No problem, Jan. It worked out all right." She gave the tall girl a convincing grin. "I'm here, ready to get to work—for a little while, at least. And I'm starving for some of that scrumptious country cooking you're always bragging about."

Jan's expressive face registered dismay and a hint of sheepishness.

"Cook's sick."

"Cook's sick," Rowan repeated blankly.

"Yes. Mae's arthritis flared up just in the last few days, and she can't get around. She's staying with her daughter." The wide brown eyes were beseeching. "Oh, Row, I wouldn't blame you if you turned right around and left, but you *did* take that gourmet cooking class, and you *were* always the one to throw a scrumptious meal together out of the scraps we had lying around, and it *looked* so easy for you. Could you possibly . . . I mean, would you . . . ?"

"Fill in for Mae?" Rowan finished the plea. "Jan, you know cooking is one of my favorite things to do, and even if it weren't, I'd be glad to help you . . . for a day or two." *Since I'm here, I suppose I can do that much,* she thought.

"It's only fair to warn you that this won't be gourmet cooking for a small dinner party; this is three hearty meals a day for at least fifteen people. And it's getting hotter . . . and more guests are coming." She gave a harried sigh as she cast unseeing eyes about the charming room, seeing only the work to be done and the obligations to be met.

"Don't fret, pal. You couldn't chase me away. I'll do what I can."

"Oh, Row, I *knew* I could count on you." Relieved, Jan regarded her fondly.

Indeed, Rowan realized, Jan had always been able to count on her, for in spite of her fragile appearance, she had never been afraid to tackle anything. This couldn't be any more difficult than that time when, in college, she had taken on the responsibility for a campus fundraiser, and had conceived and carried out a unique seated dinner for twenty-five select guests. By the last course, the dignitaries were sending compliments to the chef—and substantially increasing their donations to the school. She liked to think this same drive was responsible for her meteoric rise in the fashion industry as well.

"I don't believe in coincidence, do you, Row?"

Taken aback by the serious turn of the conversation, Rowan stammered, "I–I can't say I've given it much thought."

"I mean, here you are at last—just when I need you most—after I've practically begged you to come for years." Jan grew pensive. "There's a reason for everything. God's timing is always perfect." Shaking off her contemplative mood, Jan's eyes danced once more. "Oh, but there's plenty of time to talk later. After you've rested, I'll give you the grand tour and a rundown on the guests. Thank goodness they're in town to have dinner and to see a country-western show. It will be late when they return."

"Sounds good. And don't worry. Everything will turn out just fine. Haven't we always worked well together?" She smiled as Jan closed the door behind her.

Suddenly the door popped open again, and Jan stuck her head around the frame. "We *do* make a good team, don't we?" she said with a grin and disappeared without waiting for an answer.

"Jan, Jan," Rowan murmured, "don't ever change."

She leaned against the door and looked around the room, her eyes drawn to the ornate brass bed spread with a hand-pieced quilt. Tiny triangles in vibrant colors were scattered over the bed like blazing jewels, leaping and shimmering in the late afternoon sun.

"Oh, my," she whispered as she sat on the edge of the bed and smoothed the quilt with a reverent touch. Her fingers traced the delicate stitches that outlined each triangle, and she shook her head in amazement.

Her glance moved to the antique pine dresser, its wavy mirror casting distorted dancing images about the room. An equally old pine rocker, nested with plush pillows, beckoned the weary traveler to take heart from the magnificent view through the window. A small pine quilt chest served as a night table and held a handsome antique lamp with a beaded glass shade. Bless Jan for remembering her proclivity for reading in bed!

She sighed. Philip and Robbie would have loved it here. *But they aren't here,* a small cold voice within reminded her.

She rose to stand at the window, staring with misted eyes at the vista beyond. In the quiet room the memories flooded her with an almost physical force—memories of Philip, with whom she had shared three short years. Her knuckles whitened as she clutched the window frame. And baby Robbie, with a cowlick ridiculously like Philip's, taking his first faltering steps. Now she was alone. All alone.

She stumbled back to sink into the rocker and lean her head wearily against the headrest. The fingers of her right hand found the gold band and turned it round and round.

She ground her palms against her ears to shut out the sound of metal screeching against metal, the sound forever recorded in her brain. The screams. The pain. The slow recovery in the hospital, which became a haven shielding her from commitment or involvement.

Even God had deserted her, letting her survive the massive injuries to exist alone. For she could no longer turn to a God who would orchestrate—or permit—such chaos.

She rose from the chair and stumbled to the bed to fling herself upon it and curl into a trembling fetal ball. She burrowed deep into the pillows, a smothered moan escaping her lips. Clutching the pillows, she forced herself to lie still until the cloak of calmness she habitually wore returned.

Slowly she rolled over onto her back and stared, dry-eyed, at the ceiling where the shifting shadows frolicked. As she watched the dappled light above her, a wry smile lifted the corners of her mouth. The memories persisted—no longer of her little family, but of Neal. What a bizarre turn of events!

Here she was now, on Neal's turf. True, Jan had vowed that her brother would be away on business related to running Twelve Oaks most of the summer, but his presence stirred painful remembrances and fleeting thoughts that hadn't tormented her for years.

She could still feel his caresses and the insistent softness of his mouth on hers. The husky voice, whispering words of endearment, haunted her still. It had been his resolute determination to break her will and force her to submit to his proposal that had frightened her away. But that was the old Neal. Who was this stranger who evoked the old stirrings in her, while carefully keeping his distance? What was his game? Was he simply waiting to take advantage of her again? She might not be the same naïve girl he had known, but she was just as—more—vulnerable.

"Enough, Rowan Hayley!" she said aloud as she rose from the bed. She had to get busy. She could take only so many memories. Sometimes it seemed her whole life was made up of memories.

She began unpacking, hanging her belongings in the carved armoire. *No more running, Row,* she continued the silent monologue as she carried a stack of dainty lingerie to the pine chest. *You're not a child anymore; you're a woman now, with a successful career to fill your empty hours. You don't need any man—especially Neal Conrad!* She slammed the drawer shut emphatically.

Pulling faded jeans over her trim hips and slipping into a blue cotton knit shirt, she studied her reflection in the wavy mirror. She saw a gamine face, framed by a cloud of soft brown hair tinged with red. She ran a comb through her hair, watching her actions with clear green eyes, the halo of gray around her iris dark in the waning light. A soft coral gloss enhanced the smile she put on for Jan.

She paused for another look out the wide window. Beyond the cottages and pool, the variegated greens of the tree-clad foothills stretched to infinity, modulating from the bright green of the new maple leaves to the smoky blue of cedars and the blackish green of the pines in the distance. Remnants of white dogwood blossoms, like tattered flags, punctuated the manifold greens.

A deep notch in the hills to her right revealed the wet ribbon of the river far below, with a glimmer of golden green willows just visible at this distance. As she watched, a toylike canoe with a tiny figure at the oars slipped past the notch and out of sight.

She sighed. Under different circumstances she would be enjoying this retreat. With another wistful look about the serene room, she turned and walked slowly down the stairs.

"Oh, good." Jan looked up from some paperwork on the desk in the corner and put down her pen. "I just plugged in the coffeepot and we'll have time to look around outside before we eat. Okay?"

"Perfect. And, Jan, I love my room. It's all my childhood fantasies come true—living in a castle in the clouds."

Jan beamed. "Good. I hoped you would." She led the way out through a side door. "Let's go this way. You have an 'aerial view' of the pool and cottages from your room," she laughed, "so we'll take the path past the tennis court and horseshoe pits."

As they walked down the curving drive, Jan gestured to an open area to the left. "This is where we have our softball tournaments."

"Tournaments?"

"Oh, yes. Softball, tennis, horseshoes, any kind. Everybody plays. We usually have something going every evening after dinner. Here, let's cut through this way."

Rowan quickened her pace to keep up with Jan's longer strides. Giant oaks canopied their path, forming a cool, shaded tunnel through the woods.

"I want to show you the stables and barns, and then we'll come back by the main path."

They emerged from the woods at the west side of the stable. Painted deep barn-red with white trim, it sat on a small rise with white-fenced pastures stretching into the distance on either side. Rowan could see several sleek horses grazing nearby.

"It's picture-perfect, Jan. I'm so happy for you," she hesitated, "and Neal, of course."

If Jan noticed her hesitation, she made no comment. "The riding horses are all out to pasture, but I want you to meet Toby."

"Toby?"

Jan didn't answer, but led the way through the double doors to stand inside while their eyes adjusted to the dusky interior. Their nostrils were assailed by rich, earthy animal smells as they walked down the central passageway between empty box stalls. They entered the paddock through a low arched door. Immediately a fat, brown pony trotted over to them, whinnying a welcome.

"Hi, boy." Jan stroked the velvet muzzle. "This is Toby, Row."

"He's a darling." Rowan patted the sturdy back and was rewarded with a nuzzle, the broad head butting gently against her.

"And here's Boots." Jan reached down to pick up a huge long-haired red and white cat, obviously named for his four white feet.

"Oh, let me!" Rowan took the cat in her arms where he settled his bulk comfortably against her without blinking at the change. He rumbled his pleasure as she scratched behind his ears, fluffing up the soft fur. She was rewarded with a moist lap of the sandpaper tongue.

"I'm afraid he's spoiled. He lives in the house and only comes out for an occasional visit to the barn." Jan reached over for an affectionate pat.

"Oh, Slim," she hailed the man as he came around the corner, a sack of feed balanced on one angular shoulder. "Slim" was no misnomer, Rowan judged. He was all sinewy, corded muscle, without an ounce of fat, the faded jeans tight over the muscular legs and slim hips.

He lowered the sack to the ground and ambled over to them.

"Row, Slim helps Milo in the stables. Slim, this is my good friend Rowan, who is here for a visit—a long one, we hope."

Rowan forced a smile. "Hello, Slim."

A taciturn nod acknowledged her greeting. He looked at Jan. "Lots to do before Milo comes back," he said as he retrieved the sack of feed and went into the stable.

"Not much for conversation," Jan observed, "but he's a good worker."

They returned to the lodge by way of a broad brown graveled path cut through the woods. Jan strode ahead, leaving Rowan to stroll more leisurely, savoring the carpets of pink and white spring beauties still in bloom in the shady spots and the wild violets growing in profusion at the edge of the path. Wild blackberries reached deep red barbed stalks to catch the unwary, while bees droned about the pink-tinged white blossoms that promised plump berries in late summer.

The sun was warm on her shoulders and a deep contentment was settling over Rowan. She was beginning to appreciate the deep attachment Jan and Neal had for this place. If only . . . She shook off her momentary lapse of restraint and rushed to catch up with Jan.

Back in the spacious kitchen cold spring water quenched

their thirst after their walk and piping hot coffee and thick roast beef sandwiches satisfied their hunger.

"Ummm," said Rowan. "Do you raise your own beef cattle?"

"Uh-huh," Jan answered around a mouthful. She swallowed. "Before I forget—Neal had an emergency call to the Dallas plant. He didn't know when he would be back."

Rowan took a quick gulp of coffee, burning her tongue. Great! Now she could relax for a few days. Then Mae would come back to cook, and she would be free to leave. She really should tell Jan she couldn't stay for a prolonged period of time. She'd tell her tomorrow.

"Now," said Jan, "I promised you a thumbnail sketch of the guests and what to expect around here. Although," she gave a rueful laugh, "you can usually expect the unexpected. I guess that's why I enjoy all this so much after teaching all year. My chosen career seems dull by comparison."

"And how is the world of the classroom teacher?"

"My history students are great." Jan grinned. "And so is Bill," she said, anticipating Rowan's next question. "He's in Europe for six weeks with his history class—twenty-six teenagers! Can you imagine? You'll meet him later. Now, about the guests."

Rowan listened attentively, trying to visualize the people she would be serving. It was a mixed group, young and old, families and young singles. It shouldn't be too bad.

"Another guest will arrive tonight," Jan said in a tight voice. She drained her cup and got up to get the coffeepot, pouring them each a refill. She sat down and looked soberly at Rowan, pulling at the pigtail over her shoulder.

"Well? Are you going to tell me who it is?" Rowan asked, wondering at Jan's hesitation.

"Her name is Reva Fielding."

"And?"

"She's a friend of Neal's." Jan stared at the bottom of her cup, then raised troubled eyes to Rowan. "I know you don't want to talk about Neal, Row, but honestly," her voice quivered, "I don't know what he's thinking of, having her here!"

Conscious of an uncomfortable palpitation at the mention of Neal, Rowan met the disturbed eyes of her friend with a composure she did not feel. "Why do you say that?"

"She's all wrong for him!" Jan blurted. "I know, I know," she said, correctly interpreting Rowan's bland look, "you don't think much of Neal anymore, and that's your business. But I happen to think he deserves better than Reva. She's someone he knew before he became a Christian, and she's attractive, all right, but she's also petty, sneaky, possessive." Jan paused, abashed. "Well, you get the idea."

"She sounds like a real winner," Rowan commented dryly. "She'll be here tonight?"

"Yes. She made the arrangements before Neal knew he would be away. She decided to come anyway. Row, I hope you won't mind too much."

"Mind? Why should I mind?" she said airily.

"Well, that's a relief!" Jan mopped an imaginary bead of sweat from her brow. "Now, I'll show you where everything is here in the kitchen, and we'll plan some menus."

As they left the kitchen some time later, a commotion drew their attention to the driveway and they looked out the window to see an aged taxi coming to a creaking stop in front of the lodge.

"Uh-oh," Jan grimaced. "Here comes trouble."

As they watched, a tall, willowy blonde stepped out of the taxi with a flash of long, shapely legs. Shoulder-length champagne beige hair swung gracefully about the slender neck. Even at this distance, her simple white frock looked expensive. A white leather bag hung carelessly from one slender shoulder.

Whatever else she might be guilty of, the woman knows how to dress, Rowan admitted to herself, no doubt in her mind that Reva Fielding had arrived.

chapter
3

"REALLY, JAN, YOUR TRANSPORTATION here is positively archaic!" Reva gave her hostess a perfunctory hug, then issued orders to the driver who was removing her luggage from the trunk.

"Well, it serves the purpose, and it's cheap," Jan said lightly. She turned as Rowan joined them. "Reva, this is Rowan, my friend who is here for the summer."

Rowan's presence was acknowledged with an imperious inclination of the blond head.

"In fact," Jan winked at Rowan as Reva's gaze wandered, "she's the cook."

"Oh, really?" The cold blue eyes raked the petite figure. "Are you sure you're big enough to reach the stove?" A tinny little laugh escaped the sculpted lips.

"I manage," was the clipped response. For Jan's sake, Rowan refrained from adding a few choice thoughts of her own.

"Slim will bring your bags," Jan cut in. "I'll show you to your cottage."

"Has Neal arrived yet?"

"Neal?" Jan eyed the woman curiously. "I thought you

knew. He picked Rowan up at the airport and dropped her off before leaving on a business trip. He didn't say exactly when he'd be back, but he's usually gone at least a week or two."

"Oh, that's all changed," Reva replied coolly. "He'll be back shortly—no later than tomorrow, as a matter of fact. He called to explain." Her smug look left no doubt that she believed herself to be the reason for his change of plans.

"Well, then," Jan turned a weak smile on Rowan, "I guess we'll be seeing him sooner than we expected."

Rowan accepted her mute apology with a sinking feeling. Well, if Neal was coming back, she was leaving. It was as simple as that. Making her excuses, she retreated to her room.

She was shaking as she closed the door firmly and went directly to the closet for her bag. She opened the suitcase on the bed and, in a few quick steps, emptied the contents of the armoire and drawers. Her mind was curiously blank; her movements staccato-like. Only when she had snapped the lid shut did she hesitate, standing indecisively beside the bed.

She had to get away. In spite of her earlier resolve to face Neal if necessary, she quailed before the fact. His presence brought back too many hurtful memories. She'd have to think of some reason to explain her sudden departure.

The attempt to marshal her thoughts caused her head to spin. Call the taxi. Find Slim to carry the heavy bags downstairs. Leave a note for Jan. There. Once the decision was made, it wasn't so difficult to implement the plan after all. Rowan left the room and hurried down the steps.

She was met at the foot of the stairs by a distraught Jan. Her color was high and she was breathing heavily.

"Row, I'm going to commit mayhem!" she said wildly. "That woman's been here less than an hour and already I'm so mad, I could spit nails. 'Jan, dear, please tell the cook that I dine at seven sharp,'" she mimicked Reva. "'And, Jan, dear, I prefer a change of sheets for my afternoon nap as well as before I retire for the night.' It's going to be a long week, I can tell you!"

Her anger subsiding with her outburst, Jan sank down on the bottom step. "The sad thing is that she's very intelligent and has a terrific job as a programmer, but it's ... it's like all her worst traits, and mine, too, I guess, surface when we're together." She gave a rueful sigh. "Anyway, Row, I'm really sorry about the mixup over Neal. I didn't know he was planning to be home."

"I know you didn't, Jan. I'm not blaming you."

"It's selfish of me, Row, but I'm so glad you're here. Not just for the cooking, though goodness knows what I would do without you! But I desperately need your moral support right now." She turned moist eyes to Rowan who stood clutching the newel post. "Please stay."

Moved by her friend's distress and victim of her own empathy, she nodded in passive consent, a heavy weight lodging in the region of her heart.

Rowan awakened early, before full light. She raised up on one elbow, peering at the misty morning through gray rectangles of glass. Too early to get up, she decided. With a sigh, she turned and burrowed into her pillow, pulling the light blanket around her against the chill, determined to sleep awhile longer.

Restlessly, she sat up again and punched the pillow into a soft mound before sinking into its depths.

It was no use. She might as well get up. She swung her feet to the floor with a groan. Trying to court sleep would only result in a blinding headache. She'd make the coffee and get a head start on breakfast.

Rowan smoothed back her tousled hair. Pulling a light cotton housecoat over her short summer nightgown, she padded barefoot to the hall, the smooth floorboards pleasantly cool beneath her feet. She would come back and dress before the others were up and about.

She paused on the landing to rub her eyes and gazed out the small diamond-shaped window, which framed a few late glimmering stars and a thin, white sliver of moon vying with the red ball of the rising sun for space in the cloudless sky.

Good. It would be a clear day and not too hot. She sniffed appreciatively. The rich aroma of fresh coffee wafted up the stairwell. She made a wry face. Jan was already up.

She pushed open the swinging door into the kitchen, expecting to find her friend. Jan wasn't there, but Boots rose to greet her and circled her bare ankles, purring huskily.

"I know, boy. You're ready for breakfast, too. Let's see about some milk."

She stepped over the furry body to open the refrigerator, and took out the carton. The icy air flowed over her bare feet and sent a shiver down her back.

She turned to pour the milk into Boots's saucer and, in the eerie light from the open refrigerator, caught a glimpse of an indistinct figure standing by the back door.

She gasped, the slippery milk carton threatening to slip from her fingers. "When did you get back?"

"Very late last night," Neal replied, stepping into the circle of light.

In the dusky kitchen he loomed even larger than she remembered. She could see he was dressed for a day's work in jeans and blue workshirt. Dried mud clung to the worn boots on his feet. That he was an enigma passed through her mind—this suave sophisticate with the calloused hands and mud-caked boots.

She bent and poured the milk into the saucer, some of it splashing onto the floor, then straightened and set the carton back in the refrigerator. She stepped around Boots, who was lapping noisily at his breakfast, and turned to face Neal, carefully keeping her expression noncommittal.

He took a step nearer and stopped, standing quietly, pinning her to the spot with his eyes.

Panic was rising within her, her erratic heartbeat threatening to choke her with each thud as she stared back, mesmerized. In the strained silence she suddenly became conscious of the burp-burp of the coffeepot. She made a half turn toward the sound.

"Coffee's ready."

She was appalled to find the heavy resonance of his voice still sent chills along her spine.

As naturally as she could will her trembling legs, she walked to the cabinet and reached for two mugs. She turned her back to him and filled them, her hands shaking at the thought of having to carry off this unwelcome encounter.

She set the brimming mugs on the table, steamy clouds of vapor rising in the cool morning air, and turned toward him.

"How do you like your coffee?"

He eyed her reproachfully for a moment. "Don't you remember, Rowan? Have you really forgotten?" He pulled out a chair and sat down at the table.

She could feel the slow flush warming her face, creeping to her hairline. Of course she remembered. How could she forget the morning coffee she had so enjoyed preparing for him the times he had visited the tiny off-campus apartment she had shared with Jan?

"Feed him, will you, Row?" And Jan had blithely gone on to class, leaving them alone. And she had fed him. Delicate omelettes, crisp bacon, coffee—with a dollop of cream and precisely one and one-half teaspoons of sugar.

Nobody can make coffee exactly the way I like it except my little Row. She turned away and stared blindly out the window as the soft voice from the past swirled intimately through her brain. She gripped the edge of the counter to steady herself.

Abruptly she straightened and drew a deep breath. "Cream *and* sugar, right?" she asked shortly and thumped the containers on the table before him, causing a spray of cream to shower the table.

"Right." The white teeth gleamed beneath the mustache. He leisurely added the cream and then meticulously spooned the sugar into the caramel-colored coffee and stirred briskly.

Scarcely daring to breathe, she watched over the rim of her own mug as he drank. Slowly he lowered his cup and held her eyes across the table, a palpable tension shimmering between them.

"Nobody can make coffee quite like my little Row," he

said deliberately, his voice low and intimate in the dimly lit kitchen, studying her through narrowed eyes.

She sputtered, slammed her mug down, and shoved her chair back to stand before him, stretching to her full five feet, three inches.

"I am not *your* little Row." She ground out the words in slow, measured tones. "I believe that matter was settled on the drive down here." Unconsciously she leaned on the table toward him for emphasis. "We agreed we would be civil if our paths crossed. Nothing more."

Lazily he leaned back in his chair, cupping the mug in lean brown fingers, and returned her gaze through slitted lids.

"I don't remember agreeing to anything, little one." His voice lingered on the last words. "That was your decision."

"Mine!"

"Yes, yours." He took a long swallow of coffee and set the mug on the table. "I didn't contradict you because I realized how disturbed you still were over your husband's death. I thought perhaps you needed a little more time—" He stood and stretched, flexing the muscles across his massive chest and shoulders. "Although I think two years is long enough, don't you?"

The low voice was silky smooth, but with an intensity vibrating in the simple words that caused her heart to pound.

She whirled toward the door, wanting only to escape. How dare he insinuate himself into her life!

Swiftly he moved to head her off, light and quick on his feet, grasping her wrist as she tried to make it through the doorway.

"Let me go!" she said through clenched teeth, jerking her arm and causing the rough hand to tighten painfully. "Let me go—now!" She realized her voice was rising and struggled for control.

"Shhh. You'll wake Jan."

He reached for her other arm, and she instinctively folded it behind her. With a gasp, she realized what she had done as he encircled her slim waist and easily captured her arm, pulling her closer.

"I said, 'Let go!'"

"Hush, little one." He made no move to pull her closer.

Rowan felt the whisper of his words against her hair as she stood in the circle of his arms, fearful of moving lest those arms tighten, fighting her instinctive reaction to struggle away from him. He moved one arm away from her waist, and she stiffened, instantly poised for flight.

"Rowan, look at me," he demanded softly. His free hand going to her chin and lifting it.

She yielded to the pressure of his fingers on her chin and raised rebellious eyes. To her surprise, the gray eyes above were warm with concern, not threatening at all.

"Rowan, I'm sorry if I frightened you. Let's sit down again, okay?"

"No, I . . ." She was uncomfortably aware of his arm still about her and the feel of his fingers on her chin.

"Please?" His arms dropped to his sides. "Just for a few moments? I know you have breakfast to prepare, but it can wait."

She regarded him steadily, unable to comprehend the look in his eyes. As far as she was concerned, they had nothing to discuss.

He moved away from her to pick up the coffee pot and refill the mugs. "Come on, Rowan, let's have some coffee." He sat down and added cream and sugar to his mug, stirring industriously. "Better drink it while it's hot." He indicated her steaming mug with a wave of a tanned hand.

She hestitated, then gave a resigned sigh. They might as well clear the air. After all, what could happen in the kitchen in the morning light? Jan should be down any minute. She sat down opposite him and warmed her hands on the mug. *So go ahead and talk,* she thought caustically as she sipped the hot beverage.

He lifted his mug to his lips.

She felt him watching her as she concentrated on her coffee. Then he looked away, directing his gaze to the rising sun sending its first dim rays through the kitchen window. *Was he really at a loss for words?* she thought.

His hands tightened on the cup, as though he were fighting something. Then, long fingers combed wearily through his white mane as he resolutely turned back to her. "Jan tells me your job keeps you pretty busy."

"Yes, as a matter of fact, it does."

"Much traveling?"

She felt a flicker of amusement as she realized he was having a difficult time with this small talk. "Some traveling now, hopefully more later on."

"You have ambitions in that direction, I take it." He eyed her quizzically. "Like head buyer?"

"Yes. With European buying trips and all the attendant perks—"

"Keeping you busier than ever?"

She gave him a level look. "Busier than ever." She had a

feeling this conversation was headed in a direction she didn't care to go. She cleared her throat. "And what about you, Neal? From what Jan says, you do quite a little traveling yourself."

The look in his eyes told her that he knew she was trying to lead the conversation away from herself.

"Yes, I do. A lot more than I like—I don't like being away from Twelve Oaks so much, but—" he lifted a blue-clad shoulder in a shrug "—that's business."

"Just what is your business?" She didn't really care, and she was sure Jan had mentioned it at some time or other, but a little imp was giving her some perverse pleasure in making him continue this idiotic dialogue.

"Tool and die."

"Oh, really."

"Yes, we have two plants—one in Dallas and the other near St. Louis." He grinned at her blank expression. "Noisy, dirty factories that stamp out metal parts," he explained. "And we have contracts all over the world—which is why I'm away so much when I'd rather be . . ."

She tuned out his words as she observed him, her head supported on her hand and eyes intent on his face. Suddenly she frowned.

". . . hope to add to our string of horses—" He stopped as the line between her brows deepened. "Is something wrong?"

"No, it's just . . . you seem . . . changed somehow . . ." It was something she couldn't put her finger on, but there was a subtle difference.

"I hope so, Rowan." He seemed inordinately pleased at her words. "There have been some major changes in my life since the last time we were together." He grinned boyishly. "Besides my hair turning white, that is."

"Mmmm—no, not your hair, Neal." She tilted her head and looked at him curiously. "Something . . . I don't know . . . just different." Perhaps it was just the light in his eyes as he talked about Twelve Oaks.

"Thanks, Rowan." His tone was serious. "The major difference, of course, is that I've become a Christian." Rowan moved impatiently at his words, but he went on. "You know that Jan and I weren't raised Christian, but Bill led her to the Lord a couple years back, and she moved me to dedicate my life to him. It's a decision I've never regretted, Rowan. I have a peace inside I never had before, and someone to take my troubles to . . ." His big hand toyed with the silver spoon as he groped for the right words. "I know you're a Chrstian, too, Rowan." His gaze wandered to her slender fingers curled around the cup, the gold band glinting dully in the dim light. "I guess that's why I was so surprised at your attitude about Philip and Robbie."

"You needn't be surprised," she said sharply, bristling at the implied criticism. "In fact, you needn't think about it at all."

"Touchy, touchy," he murmured into his coffee cup as he lifted it to his lips for a final swallow. He set the empty cup on the table and moved it about, making a pattern of wet circles.

Rowan made a face as she took another drink of the lukewarm coffee and set her mug down. So much for objectivity. It was time to think about breakfast, and if Neal wanted to sit here and draw pictures on the table . . .

"Tell me something, Rowan. Why did you marry Philip? I know you dated other men, myself included, but what made him so special?"

Rowan sat up stiffly in surprise and glared at him. *Because he was such a contrast to you,* she wanted to shout. She pushed back her chair and stood looking down at him with undisguised annoyance. *Why couldn't he just let it go?*

"Why, Rowan?" he persisted, his voice husky and demanding. "I'd like to know what made him so special?" The white eyebrows arched inquiringly as he looked up at her.

Rowan gave an exasperated sigh. "Okay." She leaned on the table and nodded in mocking compliance. "You really want to know?" She favored him with a brittle smile and watched his eyes darken. "He was trustworthy and faithful—unlike most of the other fellows I had been dating." Her words were intense and explicit. "He had plans and ambitions—which did not include seducing every woman he met. We were staunch friends before we were married lovers. We *liked* each other."

His eyes flickered at her pointed words, but he didn't move, his heavy shoulder hunched beneath the workshirt as he listened stoically, elbows on the table.

"We were in love, Neal, and who knows how that really happens. And he was a Christian." Her small fist emphasized the words with short raps on the table. "We had a Christian home—he was the head of the house. He was a good—no, a great—husband." She paused. "And a wonderful father to . . . to Robbie." She choked on the words and felt the unwelcome sting of tears beneath her lids.

"It's all right, Rowan." He gently covered her clenched fist with his warm hand.

"No, it's not all right!" She snatched her hand away and stood back from the table, drawing the robe tightly about her. "They should never have died!"

"And you blame God for their deaths?"

"Who else? The Scriptures say he's all-knowing and all-powerful, that he controls everything, right."

"Yes, of course, but—"

"Then he didn't have to let them die, did he?"

He bit back the words on the tip of his tongue, stood up with a sigh, and fingered his mustache. "I'm sorry, Rowan."

"Sorry! You're always sorry!" Her voice was raspy with unshed tears. "Always probing . . ." Her voice dwindled away as she was the remorse that shadowed his eyes even as she berated him. She sniffed and pulled a tissue from the pocket of her robe to dab at her nose. A lot of good it did for him to be sorry—it wasn't his family that was gone.

Neal moved around the table to stand in front of her. He looked down at her disheveled hair as she noisily blew her nose. His smile was tender, compassionate.

Rowan was acutely aware of him as he stood in front of her but she refused to look up as she wiped her eyes. *She couldn't—she wouldn't—cry in front of him!* She jammed the tissue against her lips to stifle the sob that rose in spite of her resolve and moved toward the door.

"Don't leave like this, Rowan," he pleaded, moving around to detain her and involuntarily reaching out to her.

"No, Neal!" She moved back a step, her expression bleak. Her chin went up as she faced him. "Don't ever touch me, Neal." Her voice was thick with anger and grief.

"You can relax, Rowan," he said gently and moved back

to widen the space between them. He glanced at the clock on the wall.

She followed his glance. "I've got to get dressed and start breakfast before the hungry horde descends.

"Rowan?"

"Yes?" *Now what?*

He gave her a crooked little grin, and his hand lifted to tilt her face up to him. "One more thing before you go . . ." He bent his head to lightly brush his lips against hers, the soft bristles of his mustache prickling gently in a path across her mouth.

"And I thought you'd changed!" She ground out the words. "You haven't changed at all, have you?" Her anger mounted, and her eyes were a green glitter between narrowed lids. "The same domineering, demanding . . . Christian!"

"But I have changed, Rowan. I can never claim sainthood, but I *am* a Christian!"

"Ha!" she blurted.

"Please, Rowan, give me a chance. I know you find it hard to believe, but I only want to help. You've been through a painful time—but all of us have suffered hurts in our lives. We've all experienced losses—perhaps not as devastating as yours, but losses just the same. If I seem demanding, it's only because I feel so strongly that you are in need—not of what Jan or I, or even these Ozark hills can give you, but what God can provide. Please believe me."

Could it be that he was speaking the truth? *No!* She answered her own unspoken question. He had proven his nature six years ago. Not even God—if he really existed . . . if he cared—could change Neal Conrad.

"Let me leave, Neal. We obviously have nothing more to say to each other."

"But I think we do. Can't we be friends, Rowan?"

"I'm not your friend, Neal. It seems you pick another type of person for your friends. I'm not like Reva . . . and I don't want to be. If you need to talk to a friend, go find her. I'm sure she'll be more than willing to tell you anything you want to hear."

His calm demeanor was beginning to show signs of evaporating into anger, and his eyes held the glitter of polished steel. "Just what do you know about Reva, anyway? Have you spent any time with her? Talked to her? You may be surprised to learn that you *are* like Reva . . . in some ways. Both of you are trying to deny your need for God and his saving nature. But at least Reva doesn't try to live in the past."

"I am not like that . . . that . . . woman! And don't try to tell me I am. I told you we have nothing to discuss. The fact that you know me no better proves that."

She pushed past him, intent on escape. An agonized howl rent the silence, and she stumbled against the door jamb.

With a malevolent look over his shoulder, Boots beat a limping retreat.

Her anger broken, Rowan collapsed weakly against the wall, laughing softly, an edge of hysteria to her mirth.

Ruefully, he faced her, the crimson flush of anger fading. Then, as her laughter threatened to overcome her, he reached for her.

"Rowan! Stop it!"

The grasp of his fingers on her upper arms quickly

quieted her laughter. Her breath came in hard, shallow gasps as she stood quietly, her eyes on the floor, unable to look at him. She took a deep breath and started through the door, wanting to put as much space as possible between them.

"So we have nothing more to say to each other? I find that hard to believe."

"Believe it!" She spat out angrily, pulling her robe tightly about her and backing away.

"No. No, little Rowan, I don't believe it." Abruptly, he released her and stood back, a fine sheen of perspiration covering his face. The corded hands were clenched at his side as his eyes held hers.

She shook her tousled head to clear her senses and put a trembling hand to her throat to still the pounding pulse there as she stared back, unable to look away.

Without a word, he turned, and she gaped at his retreating back as he strode to the door. He turned back to her.

"A warning, little one. I'm praying that one of these days," he said softly, "you'll come to me!"

Then he was gone, without a look back.

"That day will never come," she whispered fiercely. "Never!"

chapter
4

A SHAKEN ROWAN doggedly prepared breakfast later that morning.

"I hate you, Neal Conrad!" she muttered, vehemently directing her anger at the pan of biscuits as she slid it into the oven and slammed the door.

"What a gorgeous day!" Jan exuded a disgusting note of good cheer and optimism as she fanned the swinging door into the kitchen. "And what were you saying?"

"Oh, nothing. Just talking to myself." Rowan looked up, her face flushed from the heat of the oven, a dusting of flour on her nose. "Are the guests ready to eat?"

"Just about. Oh, good, here's Milo!" Jan held the door for a wiry little man.

Of indeterminate age, Milo was as hard and brown as a walnut. Twinkling blue eyes peered out of a face seamed with the years. Self-consciously he removed a stained straw hat to reveal sparse sandy hair sprouting from his high-domed head.

At Jan's introduction he nodded shyly at Rowan, a singularly sweet smile lighting the faded eyes.

"Rowan is going to be our cook until Mae comes back.

She's great! I can vouch for that," Jan added at his dubious look.

"I come about that cookout this evenin'."

"What about it?"

"Be rainin' by tonight."

Both women observed the splash of brilliant sunshine spilling onto the kitchen floor, and then glanced at each other.

"Can smell it," he insisted, noticing their puzzled looks. "Air just don't smell right. Rain tonight, good storm by tomorrow, for sure."

"Milo forecasts the weather with his nose," Jan gibed gently. "But I've learned never to question his judgment. He's usually right."

"You'll see," he persisted. "Better have that hayride early."

"We-e-ll, if you really think so, Milo."

"Yep. Ain't no mistake about it."

"I suppose we *could* arrange a picnic lunch."

"Yep. That's what I'd do if I wuz you." There was no budging him. "My, my, would ya look at that!"

Awe filled his voice as Rowan lifted the pan of golden-brown biscuits from the oven. Jan reached for a plate and gingerly placed three of the steaming crusty mounds on it.

"These are all yours, Milo." She smiled affectionately at the old man as she handed the plate to him. "And help yourself to some of those peach preserves on the table. Now, Row, let's get breakfast served to the hungry horde. Thank goodness, we won't have more guests 'til this weekend." She paused in the doorway. "Neal came back late last night."

"I know," Rowan retorted.

"Oh?" Jan quirked an eyebrow. "I want to hear about *that* later." She marched into the dining room with her tray before Rowan could respond.

Following close on Jan's heels, Rowan's swift, assessing glance over the diners told her Neal was not there. Nor Reva. She let out a slow breath.

"Good morning, everyone." Jan paused at the first table and set down her tray. "I want you all to meet my dearest friend, Rowan Hayley, who's going to be our cook for a few days. She's not very big and she's a city slicker, but in spite of those counts against her, she *can* cook."

She looked down at the beaming couple seated at the table. "Row, this is Homer and Elizabeth Adams."

"Glad you're here, dear." The pink-cheeked dumpling of a woman patted her hand as she spooned out buttery eggs and slices of pink ham, the brown edges curling.

"That goes for me, too." The spare, angular husband echoed his wife's greeting. "Maybe now we'll get some good food around here," he said with a sly glance at Jan.

"As if we haven't been trying to fatten you up for ages!" Jan teased, and they moved on.

"Coffee here for the Blakes—Bill and Marie—Row, and milk for Stevie." She ruffled the child's hair beneath his red cowboy hat, and was rewarded with a mischievous smile. "And this is Lisa."

Rowan allowed herself only a brief glance at the small boy sitting at the table. His little sister, sleeping in her padded seat, somehow didn't arouse the same feelings in Rowan as did her brother. *If I had had a daughter, though . . .*

"Mark and Terri Glenn." Jan paused at the table where a young couple sat very close together. "Our honeymooners," she added unnecessarily.

Rowan acknowledged their self-conscious response but didn't linger.

Sounds of appreciation rang out as the golden biscuits, crisp fried potatoes, ham, and fluffy scrambled eggs disappeared from well-filled plates. For the first time since dawn she felt a sense of satisfaction, and her eyes brightened.

Jan tapped on a glass. "A little change in plans for today's activities, everyone. Our intrepid weather forecaster, Milo, has forecast rain for early this evening, so we'll have the cookout at the river at noon."

"With the hay wagon?" Stevie asked, with a hopeful look in the shining eyes.

"Right, cowboy. We'll load up right outside the lodge a little before twelve. Swimsuits if you like, but I'd better warn you. The water is still chilly. Now eat hearty and we'll bring refills."

Slim drove the wagon around to the door and the sleek horses stood placidly while he carried the picnic baskets and coolers from the kitchen and stowed them among the bales of hay on the wagon bed.

Rowan supervised the loading, ticking off a list of the supplies they would need by the river. She shoved the last vacuum jug in a corner and paused to dab at her face with her sleeve while she squinted at the sun already high in the sky. A trickle of perspiration ran down between her shoulder blades.

"This it?" Slim said conversationally—at least for him. He, too, was perspiring heavily as he carried out the last basket.

"That should do it, Slim," she answered. The man hefted the cooler, and Jan pulled it between two bales. "Anything else, Jan?"

"No, I think that's all." She pulled out a red bandanna and mopped her forehead. "I think we could have a cookout with no other source of heat than this sun!" "Thanks for helping load up, Slim. Milo gone yet?"

"Yep," he said shortly and climbed up to the seat. "He's got the firewood, the fishing poles, the chairs—whatever else you told him to take." He leaned over to pick up the reins.

"Can we go now, Jan?" piped Stevie as she settled him against a bale. The red cowboy hat shaded the expectant face turned up to her.

"In a minute, Stevie." Jan smiled at his impatience. "As soon as everybody gets on the wagon." Amid squeals of laughter, she reached down to help Elizabeth clamber up.

"Up you go, Mother," said Homer, providing his wife a boost. Then he swung his lean body up on the wagon and settled down in the straw with an arm around her plump shoulders.

Jan turned back to Stevie. "As soon as Reva comes, we'll be ready to go." She moved the picnic basket to make more room for her long legs. "If she ever gets here," she murmured to Rowan.

"Don't look now," Rowan gestured with a nod.

They watched as Reva sauntered to the wagon resplendent in a lavishly embroidered western shirt, crisp form-fitting jeans and glossy high-heeled cowboy boots. A white cowboy hat rested casually on the back of her head.

"There's room here, Reva," Jan said reluctantly, patting the straw beside her.

The pale eyes swept haughtily over the group seated against the hay bales. "That's quite all right, Jan, dear, but I believe I'll sit up here and help drive."

With coy titters as Slim helped her up, she appropriated the seat beside him with a smug smile on her attractive face. "Everybody ready?" She flashed a falsely brilliant smile over the wagon bed and clutched Slim's arm with a squeal as he turned the team.

Rowan gave Jan a sharp nudge with her elbow as she half-rose in anger at Reva's supercilious air. "Relax, Jan," she muttered. "We'll have a good time in spite of her," she said with more conviction than she felt. It was much too hot and sticky already and she would just as soon forget the picnic, forget Reva, forget Neal . . .

Was it only this morning she had encountered Neal in the kitchen? She felt an uncomfortable blush steal over her and caught a curious glance from Jan. Resolutely she pushed aside all thoughts of that little episode and concentrated on the scenery as the wagon rumbled down the drive.

"You okay?" Jan mumbled close to her ear.

"Fine," she assured Jan with a bright smile and focused her attention on the cloud of dust stirred up by the wagon on the gravel road. They made their way slowly on the roundabout way to the narrow sandy strip of shore bordering the river.

As they climbed down from the wagon Rowan saw that

the river was no more than a wide creek at this point, with clear water rushing over its rocky bed. Trailing golden-green willows shaded folding lounge chairs Milo had set up.

"Let's swim first, Row."

"I've got to see to lunch, Jan," Rowan demurred. She had seen little Stevie head for the beach with his pail and shovel, and just looking at him brought a new, painful rush of memories. Poor Stevie! To be rejected through no fault of his own. He was a sweet, loving child, one any mother would be proud of. But even the promise of cool water on a hot day couldn't lure her near the little boy.

"Might as well swim while I build a fire and let it burn down to a good bed of coals," Milo interjected. "Be awhile."

"He's right, Row. We've got plenty of time to swim," Jan urged. "You wore your bathing suit under your clothes, didn't you?"

"Yes, but . . ."

"No 'buts', Row. Nobody's ready to eat yet." Jan headed for a clump of willows. "Come on."

Rowan saw that Homer and Elizabeth had settled contentedly in the shade and Terri and Mark had wandered off in a world all their own. She turned from the picture of Bill and Marie already playing in the shallows with Stevie and the baby and swallowed hard as the delighted giggles of the children reached her ears.

"Coming, Jan." *This is going to be a l-o-o-ng day,* she thought, sighing as they removed their clothes and draped them over the willow branches.

"Here, Row, let me rub some suntan lotion on your

shoulders or you'll be burned to a crisp," said Jan. Her own lithe, tanned body made the smaller girl, clad in a modest black suit, look even frailer.

"Thanks, Jan."

Glistening with suntan oil, Rowan ran lightly across the sand, deliberately heading downstream away from Bill and Marie. The shock of the cold water on her feet took her breath away but she eased her way into deeper water, until she could float easily.

She saw Reva appear and tuck her hand possessively into Slim's elbow. *Poor Slim!* she thought. *That woman's way out of his league.* She was unable to suppress a little smile at the sight of the unlikely couple.

"What's so funny?" Jan sank down into the water with a shudder. She followed the direction of Rowan's gaze, and they watched as Reva moved languidly behind the hay wagon.

"Your star boarder's caught a cowboy," Rowan laughed.

Jan answered her with a snort.

"Was that a sound of laughter or disgust?" Rowan teased.

"A little of both, I guess. Listen!"

A clear, but slightly off-key soprano voice floated to them as one of Reva's fancy boots followed its mate onto a bale. Jan ducked into the water and surfaced just as Reva, in a skimpy two-piece bathing suit, paraded nonchalantly down the beach toward them.

"Poor Milo." Jan joined her laughter as they watched the old man studiously try to ignore Reva's little song and dance show. "And look at Slim!" He was kneeling by the fire and busily shoving bits of wood into the flames. "His ears are as red as the coals."

"I can't take this," Jan muttered. "Come on." With a quick flip she disappeared underneath the water's surface.

"Right." Rowan followed, gritting her teeth against the shock of being submerged in the cold water. After they became accustomed to the temperature, they swam away from shore, cleaving the water with broad, firm strokes.

"Jan," Rowan called, "I think I had better go back and see about lunch."

"I guess you're right," Jan shook her wet hair back. "Have to, sooner or later, I guess."

They made a wide circle and headed back to shore. "Oh, no," Jan groaned.

Rowan wiped the water from her eyes and followed Jan's glance. Reva was mincing along in the shallow water at the water's edge, squealing coyly.

"What a fake! Well, let's get this over with," Jan said grimly and lashed out with angry, choppy strokes.

Reva was waiting for them with a questioning pout on her full mouth. "I thought Neal would be here by now."

Rowan felt herself tense and sank down into the water as Jan faced Reva.

"Neal?" Jan's forehead furrowed. "I wasn't expecting him."

"I don't think the boss will be here," Slim chimed in, coming up behind Reva.

"Oh?" Reva frowned. "I thought sure he would."

"He said something about too much to do."

"Well . . ." Reva turned to him with a little laugh, interposing herself between him and Jan and Rowan. "In that case . . ." she gave him an arch look as she waded ashore and lowered herself gracefully to the beach towel.

Slim shook his head in answer to the unspoken invitation and ambled over to Milo.

"Close your mouth, Jan." Rowan was chuckling at the expression on Jan's face. "You have just seen a master at work. And I don't mean Reva!"

"Fire's about ready!" Milo's voice rang out over the water.

"Great," Rowan said in relief. "Come on, let's eat."

"Come on, Stevie, let's get cleaned up for lunch."

"A-w-w, not yet, Daddy."

Rowan's grin faded as she glanced at the little boy, still busy with his sand pail. She hurried behind the willow clump and put on her clothes. Maybe the meal would be a short one, and they could soon leave.

"Be with you in a minute, Row." Jan ducked behind the willows as Rowan emerged.

"I'll go ahead." She headed for the wagon. "Homer, Elizabeth, we'll eat in a minute," she told the elderly couple as she passed them sitting contentedly in the lounge chairs.

"Thank you, dear." Elizabeth smiled at her affectionately. "We'll be right there."

"Come on, Stevie," Marie called. "We're going to roast hot dogs now!"

"Yea!" The little boy threw down his sand pail and scampered ashore. "Come on, Mommy."

Rowan jerked down the tailgate of the wagon and flung on the red-checked tablecloth with trembling hands. She was breathing in shallow gasps and her forehead was beaded with perspiration. She steadied herself against the wagon and took a deep breath.

"Rowan?" Jan asked in consternation.

Rowan didn't bother to answer, but her lips thinned as she watched Jan bow her head. If Jan wanted to pray for her that was her business, but she could tell her it didn't do any good. No good at all!

The two unpacked the laden baskets and set out a bountiful meal of creamy potato salad, baked beans, and hot dogs and marshmallows to roast.

"Lemonade and iced tea here." Jan set the jugs on a flat rock.

"The watermelon! What happened to the watermelon?" Rowan looked about anxiously.

"In the river," Milo told her with twinkling eyes.

"In the river? Why?"

"To keep cold," he explained. "There, between those two big rocks." He pointed to the dark green mound just visible above the water. "Nature's icebox."

She smiled in relief. "Thanks, Milo."

"If everybody's here, we'll have the blessing," Jan announced.

"Ever'body's here that's comin', I guess," Milo muttered to her with a jerk of his head.

They all followed his glance and saw Reva disappearing around the bend in the beach.

"Does she expect us to wait lunch for her?" Jan stood with arms akimbo.

"Never mind, Jan, dear," Elizabeth soothed, "let's join hands and you say the blessing." She held out one hand to Jan and the other to Homer.

"Of course." Jan took a deep breath. "Everybody?" Everybody but Rowan. She had walked back to the wagon.

Rowan turned her back to the little group while Jan

simply and briefly gave thanks for the food. She didn't bother to bow her head, but her hands were stilled for that moment.

Chatter and laughter erupted as they held hot dogs and marshmallows on peeled sticks over the hot coals in the circle of stones, squealing playfully as the juicy hot dogs split and charred and the marshmallow puffs flared briefly and blackened.

Rowan forced a smile to her lips as she served, urging them to eat a little more, joining in the laughter as a soggy paper plate split or a cup of lemonade overturned. They were relaxed and enjoying the simple pleasure of a meal outdoors by the rippling river and Rowan envied them.

Thank goodness Marie was keeping Stevie occupied with roasting hot dogs. The baby was asleep in her basket. Rowan finally filled a plate for herself and found a spot in the shade to sit near Jan.

"Isn't this great?" Jan's dark eyes glowed as she looked at her guests.

"Great."

Jan looked keenly at Rowan, but she was carefully spreading mustard on her hot dog. She decided to ignore the note of sarcasm she was sure she had heard. "And your potato salad is fantastic, Row."

"I know," Rowan joked, "I just ate too much." She gave a mock groan and lay back with her eyes closed. She felt the knot in her stomach ease as she stretched out, eyes closed and half-listening to the banter. To her surprise, she found herself laughing spontaneously at one of Homer's witticisms.

"*Hot dogs!*" Reva's high-pitched snicker pierced the moment of fun.

Reva was glaring scornfully at the blackened hot dog on a stick that Milo was offering to her.

"I was hoping she would get lost," Jan said sulkily.

"No such luck," Rowan laughed. "I think I'll go dip my feet in the water awhile before cleaning up. Coming?"

"You're not eating watermelon?"

"You must be joking." Rowan struggled to her feet. "Not one more bite—of anything!"

She wandered down the beach and found a shady spot where she could sit on the sand and let the gentle wash of the river slosh over her feet. She leaned back on both elbows and watched the moving clouds. A few dark clouds lurked in the distant sky, but above her, cottony puffs wafted by on a gentle breeze. She closed her eyes as the cooling breeze caressed her face and the rippling water laved her feet.

"Stevie, don't bother Rowan!"

Her eyes flew open and she turned to see the little boy headed her way, the sand pail and shovel clutched in his chubby hands.

"Hi, Wowan." Guileless blue eyes met hers from beneath the brim of the cowboy hat as he advanced on her. "Wanna shovel?" He extended the red plastic shovel, a prized offering to a friend.

"Stevie, did you hear what your mother said?"

"Please, Bill, let me play with Stevie for a little while," Rowan heard herself say as her hand went out to take the shovel. Why had she said it? She would have vowed she wanted nothing less than to be in close proximity to this small boy. Stevie released the shovel and she sat looking at the plastic toy. "What'll we shovel?" she asked him lamely.

"Wanna make a castle?"

"Oh, yes, let's make a castle," she said.

Patting and digging, they soon had a sizable castle molded of the moist sand. They worked silently, the little boy intent on the slightly askew structure and Rowan gamely going through the motions in the dappled shade of the willows.

"So you *are* back!"

Rowan looked up at the sound of Jan's voice to see Neal, sitting astride a sleek black stallion and looking her way. She moved so her back was to him and busily piled the damp sand in place, mounding and shaping a turret that grew beneath her trembling fingers.

"Still plenty to eat, Boss," she heard Milo say.

"No, thanks, I'm not staying."

Good! She risked a quick glance over her shoulder and caught a sharp breath. He was coming her way, guiding the huge beast slowly between the lounging guests, speaking a few words to each.

"Wowan, look! A horse!" Stevie watched as Neal came closer, abandoning his building while he stared at horse and rider.

"I know, Stevie." She didn't turn around, but kept on working.

"Hi, Mr. Neal. I like your horse."

"Thanks, Stevie. Looks like you've been busy."

"Yeah." He turned back to the castle and picked up his pail. "Wowan's helping me."

"I see." Rowan's pale face betrayed the strain she felt, but she was putting on a good front. "Rowan? Are you having a good time, too?"

"Yes, thank you," she said shortly. She didn't look at him but went on working, shaping the turret with care, patting and piling the sand higher and higher. She could feel her face grow hot as he watched. Her hands began to tremble and a pink flush stole to her hairline. She gave an annoyed pat to the turret. To her horror, it leaned crazily for a moment, then slowly toppled, crumbling back into the grains of sand from which it was formed.

"Aw-w, Wowan."

"It's okay, Stevie," she said sturdily, her voice quavering just a little. "We'll build it up again."

"Just like life, eh, Rowan?" His words trailed behind as he cantered off, not looking back.

She leaped to her feet, furious at his meddling advice, but he was already out of range of her anger.

"Come on, Wowan, I'll help you."

The short laugh was nearly a sob as she sank back to her knees beside the castle. "Thanks, Stevie," she managed to say.

Neal nodded to Reva as he rode past, too quickly to allow her to call to him. He would talk to her later. Plenty of time to talk to her later.

He halted the horse beside Milo and ran a brown hand over his face as he looked over the languid group lounging in the shade.

"Better get them loaded up before too long, Milo. That storm isn't too far off."

"Right, Boss, whatever you . . ."

"Listen!" Neal held up a preemptory hand and the rumble of distant thunder was borne on the quickening breeze as they listened.

chapter
5

REVERBERATIONS OF FARAWAY THUNDER hung in the humid air as the lumbering haywagon pulled up in front of the lodge. The guests scrambled down, the first fat raindrops spattering around them. The resulting miniature explosions in the dusty road were soon extinguished by a steadily increasing downpour.

Jan studied the darkening, swiftly changing cloud formations with an anxious eye. "Everybody! Please keep your television sets on for weather bulletins," she called above the din as the group scattered to their cabins. "Looks like Milo may get his storm earlier than he thought."

Rowan hurriedly carried the remains of the picnic through the pelting rain to the kitchen. Jan grabbed a basket from the wagon and followed her as a loud clap of thunder echoed over the valley.

"Whe-e-e!" Jan shook back her damp hair and went into the living room to turn on the television. Rowan stood in the doorway and listened to the mellifluous voice of the newscaster.

"... a band of severe thunderstorms and heavy winds moving in a northeasterly direction at thirty miles per hour. A tornado watch is in effect for the Missouri counties of Greene, Laclede, Lawrence, Dade and ..."

"That's us!" Jan turned to Rowan in alarm.

"A tornado? Here?" Rowan's voice rose in a squeak.

"Well, just a watch so far—conditions are right to spawn a tornado. Thank God we have a storm cellar."

"We do?"

"Yes, right outside the kitchen door." She grabbed a yellow slicker from the hall closet and threw it over her shoulders. "I'm going to alert everyone and be sure they know what to do." She was gone in a flurry of gusty rain and wind.

Rowan sat down at the table and laid her weary head on her folded arms. Her nerves throbbed after the early morning bout with Neal and the cookout this afternoon. Nothing could have appealed to her more than to be able to fall into bed. But she knew the storm was going to preclude even that.

She pushed herself away from the table and mechanically began to put things away. A glance out the window showed her that the rain had diminished, but the perceptibly darkening sky caused her to shiver with fatigue and apprehension.

Rowan stepped outside on the back porch. Not a leaf stirred nor a breath of the heavy air moved. The foreboding thunder rumbled and the billowing masses of murky clouds constantly shifted, boiling from within.

A short distance from the back steps, the elongated mound of the storm cellar crouched, an impregnable refuge with a stout sloping door to shut out the raging elements. Thoughtfully Rowan studied it. She had seen such excavations before, but had never really needed one. Both its sturdy bulk and Jan's reliance on its presence gave her a secure feeling.

She clasped her arms to herself against a sudden gust of chill wind that brought goose bumps to her bare arms. The temperature was dropping quickly—a bad sign. She hurried inside.

If only Jan would return! And where was Neal? Her brows drew together and her lips thinned at the thought of him. Why, oh, why had she come here? All the hurt she thought had been laid to rest was awakened, jarred into painful memories. She paced the kitchen in agitation. And why had she been so foolish as to agree to stay even for a few days . . . Tension had honed her tingling senses to a fine edge and she whirled about as she heard the screen door open.

"Any more weather bulletins?" Jan asked as she came in.

"I'm sorry, Jan, I haven't been listening. I—I've been watching outside," she admitted sheepishly.

"No matter. I've told everyone to come here as soon as they gather up what they need. The cellar is well stocked, but you can make some coffee, okay? I'll go up and get some extra blankets."

Glad to have something to do, Rowan filled the two large coffeepots, then found the jugs they had used earlier. She pulled several large containers from the cabinet and filled them with water. What else would they need? The newscaster's authoritative voice caught her attention and she stepped to the doorway to listen.

"... several tornadoes have been sighted. No report of damage or injuries at this time. Repeating ... we are under a tornado warning. We urge all residents of the previously mentioned counties to seek shelter and take all necessary precautions. Repeating ... "

She turned back into the kitchen as Jan came in with an armload of blankets. "It sounds awful, Jan."

"I know. I heard on the radio upstairs. Would you open a couple of windows on the east side to equalize the pressure?" She went to the desk and came back with a metal strongbox, which she added to the pile of blankets.

"Let's see ... what else?" She looked around distractedly. "The appliances need to be unplugged ... "

Anxiety spurted through her as she followed Jan's directions, jerking the plugs unceremoniously from the sockets. Tornadoes were common occurrences in the Midwest and she had heard numerous warnings. But never had she been this involved in a destructive whirlwind. They could only hope it wouldn't touch down. If it did ...

"Have you seen Neal?" Jan's voice broke into her thoughts.

"What? Oh, no, I haven't." Where was he? Her face clouded with uneasiness. Now that she thought about it, it was strange he wasn't around.

"Never mind. He's probably looking after the stock. The Adamses are here. I'm going to get them settled in the storm cellar. When the rest come, please bring them in."

"Right. The coffee is almost ready. And Jan," she forced a smile, feeling the weight of her friend's responsibility, "everything will be all right."

"I know. We'll just have to take all the precautions, and then trust God. He and I make a good team, too."

Rowan poured the scalding coffee into the jugs with surprisingly speedy, but steady hands. She set them in the picnic basket and added foam cups and a carton of milk. As she paused to catch her breath, her fears grew stronger and she quickly picked up the basket to go outside.

An ominous silence greeted her as she stepped out on the porch. No one was in sight, although the doors to the cellar stood open. To the west the black clouds churned ceaselessly, the sky beneath them a curious greenish color she had never seen before. A tight knot formed in the pit of her stomach as she watched feathery black fingers separate from the boiling mass and move swiftly to converge again with the mother cloud.

At least, so far, the distinctive funnel of force that could wreak such havoc in a matter of seconds wasn't visible. She knew any one of those trailing clouds could suddenly take on a life of its own, twisting and turning, forming the whirling vortex that stretched earthward, a greedy spinning mass that snatched and gulped down anything in its path.

A measure of relief flooded over her as she saw Mark and Terri ambling down the path from their cabin, their arms tightly about each other's waist, oblivious to the threatening storm. She had once known that kind of absorption in another person—an involvement that could shut out everything but each other. The knot in her stomach drew tighter.

Thoughts of Philip always spawned thoughts of Robbie. And today, thoughts of Robbie caused her to think of Stevie Blake. Stevie! Where could he and his family be? Surely they weren't lost in the storm. Their cabin wasn't that far from the main building. *Please don't let anything happen to him!* she closed her eyes and pled to . . . *whom?*

THIS BAND OF GOLD

"Hi, Wowan." Her eyes snapped open. Stevie still wore the red cowboy hat and clutched a well-worn teddy bear, striding ahead of his parents in miniature cowboy boots. "Are you tired? Your eyes were closed."

"Hi, Stevie. Yes, I guess I am a little tired. Building sand castles with a handsome cowboy is fun, but it's still hard work. Aren't you tired, too?"

"Nope, I'm strong. Maybe you need a little nap. That's what my mommy tells me when I'm sleepy," Stevie answered as he clattered down the cellar steps. Bill and Marie followed.

The baby Lisa chortled over her mother's shoulder as Bill struggled with all the paraphernalia an infant, even one about to experience a tornado, seemed to require.

"Hurry! Please hurry," she called to them, her voice unnaturally high. "I was afraid you were lost."

"Ever try to hurry an outfit like this?" Bill asked good-naturedly. "We brought everything but the bed. And only left that because I couldn't carry it."

Marie turned anxiously to Rowan. "The weather report sounds terrible, doesn't it? Is the storm cellar safe?" Her arms tightened protectively around the baby.

"Come on, everybody!" Jan appeared in the doorway of the cellar. "Mark, Terri, this way."

The newlyweds silently disappeared into the cellar with dreamy smiles at each other. Jan stood aside for them to enter, scanned the seething blackness above them, and swallowed hard. "Come on, Row. Here, let me . . . " She took the basket from Rowan and preceded her down the shallow stone steps.

Rowan cast another fearful look at the surging clouds

before following her friend into the cellar. Roughly dressed native stone formed the walls of the cavernous interior, and the high ceiling allowed ample room to stand. Wooden benches lined the two long walls and abundant provisions sat on shelves above. Several lanterns cast their broad beams over the assembled group while a transistor radio kept them in touch with the outside world.

The room was snug and dry and cooler than outside. And comfortable—so comfortable in fact, that Stevie, despite his protests that he wasn't tired at all, curled up on one of the benches, oblivious to the fury outside and the fear inside the shelter. Rowan could almost call the surroundings cozy—if not for the touch of claustrophobia she felt. Hopefully they wouldn't be here long.

Jan was counting noses. "Now where is Reva? Has anyone seen her?" she demanded.

"Probably putting on her tornado outfit," Marie murmured to Bill.

"This is no time to make snide remarks, Marie," her husband chided her. Then he spoke to Jan. "I'm sure she went to her cabin when we did, but I haven't seen her since."

With an exasperated sigh, Jan reached for her slicker. "Be back in a minute."

"No!" Bill and Homer said in unison as they rose to detain her.

Ignoring their protests, she put her shoulder to the door and shoved against the force of the rising wind. Before they could stop her, she was gone, swallowed up in the whirling wind and rain.

"No, Bill!" Marie tightened her grip on his arm as he attempted to follow.

"Your wife's right, Bill," Homer agreed, shaking his head in dismay. "No sense in all of us running around in such a storm. If Neal were here . . . " As if in answer to his wish, the door was wrenched open and a powerful frame was silhouetted against the sinister blackness outside.

"Several small funnels have passed over," Neal announced calmly, holding up a large hand to still the frightened murmurs. "Everyone here okay?" His cool glance assessed the assembled guests, lingering briefly on Rowan's white face. His head swiveled for a second look. "Where's Jan? And Reva?" he asked sharply.

"Jan went to find Reva." Homer's voice quavered as he relayed the news. "We tried to stop her, Neal, but she wouldn't listen."

Neal glared at them in disbelief. "You mean she's out there?" The muscles in his jaw jumped as he turned a grim face to the door just as it was flung open and Slim and Reva stumbled in, rain streaming from their slickers.

"Where's Jan?" he demanded as his blazing eyes raked them.

"How would we know?" Reva said petulantly.

"She went to find you. If anything happens to her . . . "

"Well, I didn't ask her to look for me! Why would she think I needed her help? I'm a big girl; I can take care of myself!"

"I don't have time to argue with you, Reva. I need to find my sister!" With a deep controlling breath, Neal turned to Slim. "Come with me," he ordered.

A deafening roar, like that of a freight train passing through the room, interrupted him. The sound hung in the air for endless seconds, then left a vacuum of deceptive stillness. As one, the group turned wide frightened eyes to Neal, their fears for Jan and themselves naked in their mute appeal.

"I'm afraid that one touched down," Neal answered the unspoken question. As if to underscore his words, something crashed mightily against the door, splintering their fragile barrier against raging nature.

Neal put his shoulder against the door, his whole body quivering with exertion as it refused to budge. "Give me a hand," he said to Slim through clenched teeth. The two men put muscular shoulders to the door and heaved.

"Once more," Slim grunted. Again they strained and slowly the door opened as they continued the pressure.

"Part of the back porch," Neal called back as he pushed the debris aside. "Bill, Homer, come with us. Everybody else stay here until I tell you otherwise."

"But Jan?" Rowan whispered. Her nails dug into the palms of her clenched hands as she stopped in her tracks.

"We'll find Jan," he said harshly. "We don't need another one to worry about."

The suspense was killing. Why didn't Neal return? After what seemed hours, he called out the go-ahead to emerge from the storm cellar, and they stumbled out, blinking in the sudden light. When Rowan's eyes focused once more, she saw Jan sitting on the step of the roofless back porch, white-faced and still.

"Are you all right, Jan? What happened?" Her voice was high-pitched and shaky, her breathing shallow.

"Would you believe being knocked out by a piece of your own back porch?" Jan quipped weakly. "I almost made it to the cellar." She winced as she tried to move.

"You're injured, Jan! Why doesn't Neal take you to the doctor?" Rowan demanded.

"He will, Row," Jan soothed. "I'm fine right here until he gets the guests settled. Did you ever see such a mess?"

With sinking hearts they observed the devastation—shingles from the cottages littered the ground like great black beetles among the jagged pieces of wood from the porch roof. Entrance to several of the cabins was blocked by upended trees, their grotesque roots exposed.

Early dusk descended eerily under scudding gunmetal-gray clouds punctuated by an occasional silver fork of lightning. Not a bird sang nor a leaf stirred as intermittent claps of thunder rolled across the valley, accentuating the unnatural stillness.

"I hate to even look at the front of the lodge," Jan said in despair.

Neal strode down the path, followed by Bill and Homer.

"Gather 'round, everybody, please," Neal called, his voice calm and impressive in the midst of the chaos surrounding them.

They gathered uneasily, glancing anxiously toward their cabins where their possessions were—or had been.

"As you can see, we've sustained some damage." His gaze was steady as it swept over them. "At this point, it doesn't look too bad, but we don't have any electricity and all that goes with it." He paused and looked at each family. "Such as bathroom facilities, cooking, or refrigeration . . . "

"Well, I for one . . . " began Reva in a shrill voice.

Neal silenced her with a glance. "So I'm suggesting that you all pack up while it is still light enough to see and leave tonight. Fortunately, it looks as if all the cars came through without damage. I'll settle refunds as soon as possible."

"Don't worry about refunds, son," said Homer Adams. "Just be thankful it wasn't any worse."

"Thanks, Homer. And I am thankful it wasn't any worse. In fact, I'd like us all to join hands and give thanks for our safety before you all leave."

Give thanks? Rowan's eyebrows shot up. Thanks for all the damage and Jan's injuries? This whole episode was just another example of the "loving concern" shown by God—the same God who had taken her family.

Neal looked around the circle, lingering a moment on Rowan. Her nostrils flared as she glared rebelliously back at him. But his eyes were calm and compelling. Reluctantly she took Jan's hand and placed the other in the hand Elizabeth offered.

With bowed head and in a voice husky with emotion, Neal simply and fervently gave thanks for their safety.

"Heavenly Father, we thank you for sparing us from the fury of the storm. We have seen the power of nature today. We recognize that your power is greater—that you can save us not only from the death of the body but from the death of the spirit. For each life here, we thank you. Guide these travelers as they leave us. Go with them and continue to protect them. And for those of us who remain, we ask strength for the days to come—physical strength to do the necessary work and spiritual strength to keep us from despair. You know our needs; we praise your name for your blessings. Amen."

In spite of herself, Rowan was impressed by the sincerity of his gratitude. How could he be thankful, when his dream of a summer resort had been shattered? This summer was over, in effect. The damage was so heavy that the remaining days of the season would be filled, not with picnics and swimming parties, but with work and workmen.

As the guests dispersed, Neal carried Jan to the couch in the keeping room. "Now, stay there, you hear me? As soon as I check on Milo and Slim, we'll get you to town and the doctor."

"Neal, I don't need a doctor!"

"Of course you do. Now stay put," he ordered. "Rowan, stay with her." His tone brooked no nonsense from either of them.

"Yes, sir!" Rowan said mockingly to his retreating back. She looked at Jan where she lay on the couch. Of course she would stay with her. She was terribly pale beneath her scrapes and bruises and her every move obviously caused her pain.

A soft knock on the door frame captured Rowan's attention for the moment. There stood Homer and Elizabeth Adams, flanked by Mark and Terri. "Just wanted to let you know we're packed up and ready to leave," Homer said. "But we thought we'd check on Jan before pulling out. How is she?"

"I'm all right, Homer," Jan spoke up from across the room. "I'm sorry about your vacation . . ."

"Now, don't you worry about us, honey," Elizabeth interrupted her. "Maybe we should stay, Homer. Looks like these gals could use some help. If it weren't for the fact that we need to check on things at home, I'd not even consider leaving. But we've got family that'll be worried about us, and with the phone lines down . . ."

"Now, Elizabeth, you do what you have to do. We

certainly understand," Rowan told her. "I don't have a reason in the world to hurry back to Chicago. I can stay with Jan as long as she needs me." *What am I saying?* she suddenly thought. *I don't want to stay here. But Jan can't be deserted now. She'd do the same for me.*

"Well, if you're sure you'll be all right . . ."

"Of course we will. Now you better get started. You have quite a drive ahead of you. And you, too, Mark. Don't linger too long. Try to salvage some of that honeymoon."

"Well, one thing's for sure," Mark answered. "A lot of couples may have had more exotic settings for their honeymoons, but I'll bet not one can claim more memories!"

"Probably not," Jan chuckled softly. "Just recommend Twelve Oaks when you get home as the place to go for excitement. We're going to need the business—someday, when all this is cleaned up again."

Bill and Marie and their small family had joined the party gathered in the keeping room. "Bye, Wowan," piped up Stevie. "Mommy says we have to go home because of the rain. I wish I could stay and play with you some more."

Tears stung the backs of Rowan's eyelids. "Bye, Stevie. You be a good boy and maybe someday we can build another sand castle."

"I'll miss you," she added, as they turned to leave, suddenly realizing it was true. And maybe she should be thankful, too. The tornado, even with all its destructive force, had also been constructive. When she believed Stevie was lost in the storm, and while the wind was at its worst, she realized, she had not once thought about Robbie—or Philip. Maybe Jan was right; maybe the Ozarks did possess some healing power. But she still had the problem of Neal Conrad.

The sounds of the departing cars faded into the distance. But quiet reigned for only a few moments.

"Jan? Oh, there you are!" Reva stuck her head in the doorway. "Jan, dear, I'm leaving. This certainly hasn't been much of a vacation. Seems to me you'd have warned your guests of the possibility of a tornado. Hardly fair to get us out here for this. But, never mind. Just tell Nealey to call me, will you?" she ordered. She fluttered her fingers in farewell as she swept, tornado-like herself, out the door.

Jan raised up on her good elbow to look at Reva's retreating back, and then raged, "Did you *hear* her? She holds me personally responsible for a freak of nature— thinks I planned a tornado, just to spoil her fun!" Suddenly her anger was transformed to incredulity. "Nealey?" she repeated in disbelief, her voice rising on the diminutive. She winced and stifled a groan as she sank down again, a spasm of pain pinching her ashen face.

"Jan!" Rowan knelt beside the couch in alarm. "Is there something I can do?"

"No, thanks, Row." She gave her a weak smile. "I just need to get my leg moved a little . . ." She used her left hand to push her leg into a more comfortable position. "There," she grunted. Her head fell back to the pillow as she caught her lower lip in her teeth.

Rowan rose and stood over her in exasperation. "Don't try to be stoic," she scolded, her voice sharp with worry. "You need a doctor. I'm going to go find Neal." She strode to the door but stopped with her hand on the handle as Jan spoke.

"Row, he'll take me to town as soon as he can," she said reasonably. "Please, will you get the lamp down from the mantel and light it?"

"The lamp?" She was diverted by Jan's request.

"The kerosene lamp with the blue flowers, right on the end." She pointed to the mantel. "It's ready to light. Just set it in the middle of the table and take off the chimney."

Following Jan's directions, she lit the lamp with some trepidation and adjusted the wick, then carefully replaced the glass chimney. "There," she said with satisfaction as the blazing wick cast a golden pool of light over the polished table.

"Good, Row," Jan managed a smile. "You could learn to live in the hills very easily."

"No way!" Rowan declared. "I prefer to flick a switch. This is just a little too rustic for my taste."

Jan was lying quietly with her eyes closed and breathing evenly. The flickering lamplight cast shadows on her pale face.

"Jan?"

"I'm still in here, Row. Really."

"You don't look good to me," Rowan said bluntly.

"Gee, thanks." A wan smile curved her lips.

Rowan stood up decisively. "Just lie still while I find Neal." Her mouth twisted wryly. Never would she have believed she would have sought him out, but then, she had never before been in a tornado, either.

"No, Row." Jan rallied and her voice held a spark of her usual spunk in spite of the pain. "He'll come as soon as he can." She grinned triumphantly as they heard his booted feet on the porch. "Like right now . . ."

His masculine presence filled the lamplit room and Rowan felt an overwhelming relief wash over her as he took charge.

"Sorry it took so long, Jan," he said apologetically. "You holding on?"

"Yes—Nealey," she fibbed gamely.

He knelt beside her and laid a broad hand on her forehead. "Nealey? Is she a little feverish?" He glanced up at Rowan.

"I wouldn't be surprised," she snapped. Her green eyes were hard as they met his concerned look. "She needs a doctor."

He rose to tower over her. "I'm well aware of that," he rasped, his eyes like slate. "I got here as soon as I could."

"And that's not soon enough!" she retorted tartly.

"Hush, you two," Jan sang out. "Quit fighting over the body."

"Boss here?"

"Oh, Milo." Rowan went to the door as the old man spoke from the porch. "No, he isn't. He took Jan to the doctor." She held open the screen door. "Come on in."

He sat down with a sigh, his seamed face gray with fatigue.

"Are the horses all right?" She hadn't given any thought to the animals in her concern for Jan. "Were the stables damaged?"

"Ever'thing's okay out there."

"Good." She rubbed her temples to ease the beginning throb of a headache.

"Horses are a little spooked, though. Slim's still in the barn to quiet them down."

"How bad is it really, Milo?" She stirred uneasily in her chair as he hesitated.

"Well, bad enough," he acknowledged. "But could be worse. Mostly trees down. And the power lines. Might be days before the electricity is back on."

"Days?"

"Yep. Three, four. Maybe more, if the lines are down all over the county. And I suspect they are."

"So what do we do in the meantime? I mean for cooking and water and all . . . ?"

"Well, we cook what we have to on the woodstove in the summer kitchen. Pump water at the well—and follow the path to the little house for other necessaries . . ." He grinned as comprehension flooded her expression.

"You mean—the little house in the grove?"

The faded eyes gleamed in mischief. "Can't miss it. Prettiest little half-moon decoratin' the door you ever saw."

With a sinking heart, she realized he wasn't joking. Well, tomorrow she would leave, too, after she found out how Jan was. In the meantime, she was starved, and surely the others were, too.

"Might as well see if there is any dry wood in the leanto," said Milo, following her train of thought. "Cuppa' hot coffee would set right about now."

"Good. I'll see what else I can find. Do you think they'll be back soon?"

"Hard to say. Doc's probably pretty busy tonight."

Rowan was still sitting in the big chair with a cup of coffee, in reverie over the day's events when Neal carried Jan in and laid her on the couch. Rowan jumped up, instantly alert.

"Jan, you *are* hurt!"

"Just a little," she murmured drowsily. Awkwardly, she shifted the cast on her right arm and the cast from ankle to knee on her left leg trying to find a comfortable spot.

"I can't believe they didn't keep her in the hospital!" She raised incredulous eyes to Neal. "What did the doctor say?"

"She's all right; just drowsy from the shot they gave her. They didn't have room in the hospital for a couple of broken bones." His eyes were bleak as he looked at Jan, already sound asleep. "The hospital is full of seriously injured and the death toll is going to be high, I'm afraid." He dropped into the overstuffed chair and leaned back wearily.

"How about some hot coffee?"

"Coffee? Where did you . . . ?"

"Good, hot coffee, thanks to Milo. He built a fire in the cookstove. I'll get you some—and maybe something to eat. Would you like that?"

"I certainly would. I've been too busy to think of eating."

She stepped into the kitchen and prepared a tray with a mug of coffee and a thick roast beef sandwich. She carried it to the door to the keeping room and paused. *He looks so tired!* The mellow light from the kerosene lamp played over the broad planes of Neal's face, which indeed was lined with fatigue and bristled with a stiff new beard. The mane of white hair shimmered with streaks of silver. Her eyes softened and she felt a pang of regret at his misfortune. Business had seemed to be going so well. And Jan would be unable to help for some time. . . .

"Thanks, Rowan."

She flushed with annoyance when she realized he had been watching her. "Here's some food. I'm going on upstairs now," she said abruptly and turned to leave, then had second thoughts. "Or should I stay with Jan tonight?"

"No, she's asleep for the night, but I'll stay right here, just in case." His low voice was hesitant. "Rowan, I know you're anxious to leave, but . . . could you stay a few more days until I can get someone to help Jan?"

He couldn't have known about her conversation with Homer and Elizabeth, yet . . . Her heart sank. She really didn't have much choice. "I'll do what I can as long as *Jan* needs me," she said with more resolve then she really felt. She supposed she could stand it a few more days.

chapter 6

A HEADY BLEND OF WOOD SMOKE, pine cones, and rich coffee greeted Rowan as she walked along the passage to the summer kitchen early the next morning.

"Mmmm, what smells so good?"

Milo turned from the stove where he was feeding it slender sticks of kindling. "Seasoned apple wood, a few pine cones. And no better coffee anywhere than in a granite coffeepot."

"Boss says," he continued as he adjusted the damper, "we'll be in for breakfast in a bit."

Did Neal really expect her to cook on this black monster?

"Just ask Jan if you need any help."

"Sure. Thanks, Milo," she said weakly as he left.

"Use the cast-iron spiders for the bacon and eggs, Row," Jan instructed from her couch. "The fire is hotter over the firebox, so you'll have to allow for that. That little door at the top is the warming oven, so you can put the bacon up there as you fry it." She laughed at Rowan's skeptical look.

"It really works, Row. Some of the hill people here

wouldn't trade their woodstoves for all the electric ranges or microwaves in the world." She became serious. "I'm really sorry about this, Row. It's a hot, dirty job and you shouldn't be expected to do it. As soon as Neal can get someone . . ."

"It's not that I mind, Jan. I just don't know if I can do it. But," she forced a grin, "nothing ventured, nothing cooked. Right?"

"Right." She squirmed to ease the cast on her leg. "And, Row," Jan grinned as Rowan started for the kitchen, "you might as well slice up a few potatoes to go with the eggs and bacon. And the flour for biscuits is . . ."

"Enough! Enough!" Rowan groaned in mock despair and fled down the passageway.

Her despair increased as she looked at the black beast crouched in the kitchen. Tentatively, she approached it and lifted one of the round lids on the top and cautiously poked in several sticks of wood. They flared nicely and she replaced the lid.

"Now, burn, you!" she ordered.

Much to her surprise, the bacon was soon sizzling in one spider and the potatoes in the other. She had just slipped a pan of biscuits in the oven when she heard the men come in.

Neal paused in the doorway. "Need any help?" A trace of amusement tinged his voice.

"No, thank you," she said sharply, tense with the effort of preparing the meal. He could just stay out of her kitchen! "Everything is under control."

His mouth quirked with a suppressed chuckle, but he merely shrugged and went in to the table.

They sat around the old pine table in the keeping room where a pleasant breeze stirred the gingham curtains. *Thank goodness it's cooler here,* Rowan thought, as she served the men. The kitchen was an oven on its own accord by the time breakfast was ready.

Satisfaction glinted in her eyes as she surveyed the table. Not bad! The bacon was crisp; the eggs slightly overdone, with edges like brown lace. A few of the potatoes were just the safe side of burnt, but no one seemed to notice. Even the biscuits weren't bad, just a little lopsided and browner on one side. The glass dish of strawberry jam glowed from the center of the table and the rich, homemade butter was beginning to puddle in golden swirls.

Milo and Slim ate systematically, rarely looking up from their plates as Rowan quietly replenished the platters and refilled coffee cups.

Neal ate more slowly, savoring each mouthful. *Rowan's emotional problems haven't seemed to affect her cooking,* he mused. He felt a warm glow inside watching her move around the table and recalling her playing with Stevie at the beach.

He smiled to himself as he buttered another steaming biscuit. He had never thought he would be thankful for a tornado—but it alone was keeping Rowan from leaving.

He looked at her flushed face, reddened from the heat of the cookstove. He had had no intention of letting her work that hard. With luck, the power would be on in a few days. Then would she stay?

"Rowan, this is delicious!" exclaimed Jan from the couch where she leaned against plump pillows and ate from a tray. "Now I know how the decadent Romans felt," she laughed as she popped a crisp slice of potato into her mouth. "Bring on the dancing girls!"

Laughing at her nonsense, Milo and Slim excused themselves. Neal lingered, idly chatting with Jan and sitting at the table while Rowan ate her breakfast.

Glad for the chance to sit down and cool off, she didn't join in the conversation, but sat comfortably, dunking a tea bag in her mug and looking around the keeping room.

An old-fashioned combination of family room, dining room and kitchen, it had been restored and decorated as handsomely as the rest of the lodge for their own use. Shafts of sunlight gleamed on the tawny pine floors and picked out the varied colors of spongeware displayed in the antique hutch. An immense fireplace of old soft brick filled one wall, its crude log mantel laden with a collection of primitive cooking utensils. A wooden butter churn sat beside the hearth.

Rowan's eyes were drawn to the Lone Star quilt on the wall behind Jan, admiring the painstaking craftsmanship, before her attention was caught by a low moan from Jan. She started to rise from her chair. "What is it?"

Tears glistened in Jan's eyes. "Neal just said that two of the old oaks lining the driveway are down. There's nothing we can do?" she asked him hopefully.

"No, Jan, I'm sorry. They're gone, completely uprooted, just like the ones in the back. I guess we could plant some in their place, but they would never catch up in size in our lifetime. Somehow, it wouldn't be the same," he said sadly. "These were planted by some homesteader when he put up the first log cabin here. But, whatever you think . . ."

"I think, brother dear, we'll just have new brochures printed," she said teasingly.

"What does that have to do with anything? Besides, we have plenty."

"But *Twelve* Oaks Resort no longer exists. Welcome to *Ten* Oaks, Row!"

Rowan had listened to their conversation in disbelief. She had to admire their resilience, but after all . . .

"As far as the cabins go," Neal was saying, "almost all the roofs have some damage, and number twelve is completely destroyed. I hope to salvage some lumber from that. Other than that, it's mostly wet bedding and furniture to haul out and debris to pick up." He stood up and stretched, expanding his vast chest. "None of which is going to get done if I don't get out there and get busy."

"Oh, if only I could help!" Jan complained. "I could help pick up, Neal."

"You, dear sister, shall play the Fine Lady until the doctor says otherwise. Understand?"

"But it's not fair, Neal! You can't do it all."

"Can't I help?" Rowan heard herself saying.

Neal turned in the doorway and looked at her in surprise. "You *are* helping, Rowan. Cooking and staying with Jan."

"I know. I'll do that, too. But I can do whatever Jan would do." Why in the world was she pleading to do his dirty work? She looked up at him with a little twisted smile, aware of her own foolishness.

For a moment he studied the delicate face turned up to him, his own eyes impassive. "You're on, Rowan." His face creased in a smile. "I can't afford to pass up a willing pair of hands." They could hear him whistle an aimless tune as he walked down the path.

"Oh, Row, look at your hands!" Jan exclaimed in dismay.

"I know," Rowan said wryly. She held out her hands and examined them critically. "These hands, dear friend, are the hands of a working woman," she announced dramatically. "See here the broken nail, here a burn from the black beast in the kitchen . . ."

"If only I could help! You shouldn't be doing everything. I'm really sorry it turned out this way, Row."

"Don't be, Jan. Maybe this change of pace is what I needed. I know I'm sleeping better!"

"Sheer exhaustion."

"Probably. But a peace, too, Jan."

"I knew it! I told you the Ozark hills would do that!"

"Now, Jan," Rowan said good-naturedly, "don't start in on your hills."

They both looked up as Neal came in and leaned wearily against the door jamb. He wiped his face on his sleeve, leaving a dark stain.

"Rowan says the hills are working their magic!"

"Jan, I did not!" she laughingly protested.

His triumphant laughter, deep and rich, filled the room. "I knew it!" he gloated.

"You two and your hills! I'm going back to the kitchen!" She fled his disturbing masculinity. He had said nothing to upset her since they had been working to clean up the debris; in fact, he had hardly spoken to her at all.

Her muscles had begun to protest the unaccustomed strain, and for what? Did anyone, except Jan, appreciate her efforts? Probably not; certainly not "the boss." He expected everyone to work from morning to night. Well, it was her own fault. She *had* offered to help.

As soon as she put a pot of soup on the back of the stove to simmer all day, she would go back out to help. She straightened up to ease the pain between her shoulder blades. By the end of next week—if she lasted that long—she could leave.

Then let him do his own cooking! She gouged at the eye of the potato she was peeling. And his own cleaning! She jabbed at another eye.

"Ouch!"

She turned to see Neal in the doorway. "What did you say?" she asked testily.

"All I said was 'ouch'." He grinned, laughter twinkling in his eyes. "I'm just glad it was the potato, not me, you were jabbing at."

The look she gave him left no doubt she wished it *were* him. She kept her back to him while she continued, but was uncomfortably aware of him standing behind her and watching every move.

He stood quietly, smothering a grin at her vehemence. How much better she looked than when she arrived! Though she no longer looked the fashion plate, she was tanned and had probably even put on a few pounds. Most of all, she seemed less haunted—more at peace with herself, although that could be pure fatigue. He certainly was exhausted himself by nightfall. He had tried to stay out of her way because he knew his presence annoyed her, but he did allow himself the luxury of watching her.

"Here, let me do that!" In swift strides, he was beside her as she added wood to the stove, taking the small log from her.

"Never mind! I can do it," she protested, but relinquished it to his grasp.

"I know you can do it, Rowan. You've been doing a great job."

She raised a quizzical eyebrow.

"I know you're doing it for Jan, but I appreciate it, too." The gray eyes were steady as they looked into hers. "But you're working too hard, Rowan. Just tend to the cooking and Jan."

She pushed the damp hair back from her face. "I'm strong enough to do my share—Jan's share—outside cleaning up."

"You stay in here, I said," he said sternly. "Look at your hands."

She winced as he grasped her hands, the burn smarting at his touch. His large brown hands turned hers over.

"I feel guilty, Rowan, when I look at your hands." His fingers stroked the calluses in her previously soft palm and lightly touched the angry welt from the stove. "The power should be on again soon, probably today, and you won't have to cook on the woodstove."

"There's no need to feel guilty, Neal." She tried to pull her hands away, disturbed by the firm pressure of his hands. "I'm just careless."

His grip tightened as she raised clear green eyes to face him. "Rowan . . ." His voice was soft but insistent.

"I have work to do, Neal," she said quickly, avoiding his eyes. "I'll get the rest of the wet bedding out of cabin three as soon as I finish here."

He released her hands and towered over her. "No, you won't, Rowan." His voice hardened. "It's much too hot." And, besides, as much as he loved having her around, today it would be better for them both if she stayed inside with Jan.

"It's not that hot today," she argued. *Admit it, Row, you enjoy watching him.* Physically, he was a magnificent man. Milo and Slim also worked shirtless, but paled in comparison. It was hard not to be aware of the difference.

"Stay in the house, Rowan." His voice rang with finality as he left the kitchen.

"Do your own work then. Who cares!" She realized she was still holding a potato and with a mighty heave threw it after his retreating form.

It made a satisfying *splat* against the doorframe.

Neal could fuss if he wanted to, but she wanted to finish the dirty job of the cabin nearest the house. Besides, the sooner things were repaired, the sooner she could go home. She would drag out the rest of the wet bedding and drapes and clean up the best she could so the men could do the outside labor when they got around to it.

With Jan settled for a nap, she stepped from the shaded porch and saw that Neal and Slim were busy on the roof of the cabin on the far side of the drive. She walked quickly across the yard and up the step to the cabin.

Rowan caught her breath and wrinkled her nose as the

sour smell of wet bedding greeted her. A shaft of sunlight through a damaged corner of the roof gave enough light for her to survey the damage. She stood with her hands on her hips and looked around, breathing shallowly through pinched nostrils.

Apparently the only structural damage was the hole in the corner of the roof. But it had allowed the blowing rain to saturate the bedding and rug and the drapes on the window beside the bed. Well, she could drag all that out to dry and the men could carry out the furniture and mattress. She pursed her lips and shook her head, wondering if the smell would ever leave.

She bent down to grasp the corner of the large blue area rug, intending to carry it. But the sopping mess was heavier than she could handle. Rowan grunted and tugged and it slid across the floor, leaving a watery trail across the varnished wood.

She backed out the door and down the step, giving a hard pull with both hands with each backward step until the rug lay in a heap in the grass. She bent down and spread the rug on the grass, pulling at the corners until it lay square. It would have to dry like that, she decided, bending her head to wipe the perspiration on her upper lip on her sleeve.

From the corner of his eye, Neal caught a movement at the cabin near the house. With hammer raised he paused and watched with narrowed eyes. A grin widened beneath the mustache as he saw a small denim-clad form, backing down the step and into the yard, straining to pull a heavy rug. He frowned. It was much too hot for Rowan to be working and he had told her to stay inside.

He realized Slim had stopped working and was watching him, a wry smile on his sunburned face. "Go on back to the barn and see if Milo needs any help," Neal ordered as he reached for another shingle.

"Right," Slim answered. "I'll be through with this section in a minute."

"Now!" Neal's voice crackled across the yard.

Slim turned without another word, his knowing eyes flickering from his boss to the girl in the yard as he nimbly scurried down the ladder.

At the sound of Neal's voice, Rowan turned and saw that he stood on the roof watching Slim saunter toward the stable. Only when the hand reached the path through the woods did Neal squat down and resume his work on the roof, pointedly ignoring Rowan's presence.

I wonder what that was all about? She shrugged and went back in to haul out the wet drapes, half dragging and half carrying them to spread on the grass near the rug. She smothered the groan that rose to her lips as her back protested the heavy work, rising awkwardly with a hand at the small of her back. She would bring out the bedspread and then quit. Jan would be awake soon and might need some help.

Neal watched as she rose, her gestures telling him as clearly as words that she was doing too much. He stood, his spread legs balancing him as he cupped his hands to his mouth.

"Rowan, go on back to the house!"

She looked up to see his broad shoulders silhouetted against the sky, irritation in his very stance as he looked across the yard at her. She made no move to go, debating whether to finish with the wet bedclothes.

"Now!" To his surprise, she turned and began wearily climbing the steps to the back porch without a backward glance.

"My, my, aren't we bossy today?" she muttered as she opened the back door. A quick glance over her shoulder showed Neal still watching her. Well, let him think she was being docile. She still had the evening meal to serve and dishes to wash. She sighed and brushed back a wet tendril from her forehead.

"Did you say something?" Jan sat at the kitchen table carefully spooning peach jam on a thick slice of homemade bread. She took a bite as she looked up at Rowan.

"Just talking to myself." She leaned against the door jamb and watched Jan as she took another bite and solemnly chewed. "Where did that bread come from?" she demanded.

Jan deliberately spread another dollop of jam on the last bite before answering. "Mrs. Parsons sent it over," she said, waving the morsel toward the counter where two huge loaves sat in crusty splendor. "The peach jam, too." She popped the last bite in her mouth and leaned back, satisfied. "Have some, Row. It's delicious."

"I'm sure it is." Rowan dropped into a chair and cradled her head on her arms crossed on the table. "I'll eat some for dinner," she mumbled.

Jan sat up, the cumbersome cast scraping on the floor, and looked closely at Rowan. Her dark eyes were clouded with concern as she noted Rowan's flushed face and perspiration-soaked shirt. "Poor Row! You look whipped."

Rowan sat up and let her head loll on her neck, rotating

it to ease the tight muscles. She forced a grin at Jan. "Just a little stiff."

"Oh, Row," Jan wailed. "I hate it that you have to work like that. I should be doing all that cleaning." She turned a disgusted look on her leg cast. "If it wasn't for this thing . . ."

"And the one on your arm," Rowan reminded her. "Don't be silly, Jan. I *am* hot. I *am* tired." She stood up and moved to stand beside Jan. "But I'm glad I'm here to help." She gave her a quick hug and went over to the stove.

She lifted the lid on the pot of soup she had made earlier and gave it a stir. It had simmered down nicely over the banked fire and sent an appetizing aroma across the room.

"Smells delicious." Jan sniffed appreciatively and watched as Rowan lifted the stove lid and poked several slender lengths of kindling into the firebox. "That old stove, Row! You'll get overheated using it." She struggled to her feet, holding onto the table for support. "Go on outside and sit in the shade, Row," she pleaded. "I'll keep an eye on the soup and set the table for dinner, then you can take over."

Rowan smiled at her earnestness. "I'm fine, Jan. And you're the one who should be sitting down. Or better yet, lying down." She shoved the big granite coffeepot to the front of the stove. "Besides, I'm too restless to sit in the shade," she explained as she took a stack of plates from the cupboard and carried them to the table. And it was true, she thought. As tired as she was, the restlessness kept her going all day. She paused to wipe her face inelegantly on her sleeve.

"See!" Jan hobbled around the table and took the plates from her. "You're going to get overheated and Neal is going to . . ." She looked at Rowan ruefully.

"Neal is going to do what?"

"I was just going to say he would have a fit if I let you do too much in the kitchen. That's all. Honest," she said at Rowan's skeptical look. "So do me a favor, will you, Row? Sit down. Or lie down." Her face lit up as an idea struck her. "Or you could do what I do when I feel restless and need to relax."

One eyebrow rose in question. "Which is?"

"Take a walk—" she rushed on at the look of dismay that crossed Rowan's face "—through the woods to McGreevy's meadow where the wild strawberries grow."

"I don't know, Jan, in this heat," she demurred. "And should I pick strawberries?"

Jan chuckled at the look on Rowan's face. "No, you don't have to pick strawberries, Row. It was just a thought." She dropped heavily into a chair, her cast sticking straight out. "It's cool in the woods, though. And peaceful." She groaned as she tried to get comfortable. "I wish I could go myself."

"I bet you do." Rowan commiserated with her, instantly sympathetic. Jan was not a complainer, but she had to be uncomfortable. "I'll tell you what, Jan. I'll take a walk if you'll promise to lie down while I'm gone. Okay?"

Jan eyed her with suspicion. "That's blackmail, Row."

"I know." She grinned. "Deal?"

Jan grinned back. "Deal. And the berry buckets are on the middle shelf in the pantry." She held up a hand to ward off Rowan's protest. "Just in case you decide to pick some for dinner."

"Okay, okay. I'll take a bucket. Now how do I get to . . . where? McGreevy's meadow?"

"Right, McGreevy's meadow. Just go down the drive to the softball diamond and turn right behind home plate on the path that leads into the trees. It'll take you right there."

chapter 7

ROWAN FOUND THE PATH WITHOUT difficulty and slowed her pace once she entered the shaded dimness of the woods. She took a deep breath and her tired muscles began to relax as she ambled along swinging the berry bucket.

It felt good to be alone, away from the kitchen, away from the destruction around the cabins, even away from Jan's chatter for a while. And away from Neal's watchful eyes. He seemed to be everywhere, no matter what she was doing.

She scuffed through the wet leaves on the path and breathed deeply of the smell of wet earth after a rain and the musty odor of last winter's fallen leaves, caught now in molding piles among the oaks and hickorys. Her ear caught the twittering and scurrying of unseen woodland creatures punctuated by the shrill cries of the blue jays that flitted above her head.

Rowan stood still and closed her eyes, the swinging berry bucket stilled, and let the peace of the woods wash over her. Suddenly she stiffened as an alien sound intruded, causing the blue jays to swoop away with frenzied cries.

Her eyes flew open and she stood motionless for a long

moment, ears straining toward identifying the faint disturbance, but it was not repeated. She turned her head, searching the path behind her—empty, with the sun-dappled shade undisturbed. A pair of cardinals settled calmly on a nearby limb, bright splashes of color in the shadowy greenness.

Rowan let out a deep breath with a shaky little laugh at herself and moved on. *My nerves must be more on edge than I thought,* she taunted herself, but she quickened her pace until the trees thinned and she emerged on the edge of a grassy meadow that sloped away to meet a dense copse of slender hickory some yards away.

McGreevy's meadow was a shaded bowl with the late afternoon sun already behind the trees that surrounded it. The tall grasses moved languidly in the errant breeze and clumps of brown-eyed Susans nodded limply on the slope. Rowan walked through the grass and stopped abruptly as she spied a strawberry nestled in the grass.

She picked it and popped it into her mouth. She smiled as she bit into the sun-warmed fruit and felt a curious lightening of her spirit as the tranquil scene worked its magic.

A patch of late strawberries spread just beyond her toes, and she squatted down for a few more. Unconsciously she hummed an aimless tune as she picked, the plump berries dropping into the bucket with a resounding plop.

Her mind was pleasantly blank and she was totally absorbed in the mundane task when a breathy neigh sounded behind her. She looked up to see Neal emerging from the woods astride a sleek chestnut mare.

She grimaced. Couldn't she get away for even a few

minutes? The euphoric spell broken, she watched with hostile eyes as the mare daintily came toward her, her rider looking down at her with a tentative smile.

"Jan wondered if you found the meadow okay," he said rather lamely, perhaps in deference to her obvious hostility.

"You can tell her I did," she responded pertly and turned her back to him to continue picking. Her hands trembled just a little as she parted the tall grass to expose the scarlet globes. Rowan became conscious of her thudding heart as the silence lengthened. Had he left as silently through the woods as he had come?

She looked over her shoulder as casually as she could and saw that he had dismounted and was lounging in the soft grass. She turned quickly as he looked her way.

"Finding any?"

"A few," she muttered without turning around.

She moved on to another small patch and picked silently, her back to him. She relaxed a little, caught up in the quest for a few prizes hiding in the grass. Maybe if she ignored him he would leave.

He reclined on the gentle slope, propped up on one elbow as he watched from hooded eyes her hunt for the elusive treats. He was a little surprised at her short responses, but his eyes softened at the petite figure hunched over the berry patch, the graceful movement of her tanned arms a pleasure to watch.

Her size had nothing to do with her ability to work, he had decided. And under the most primitive conditions—the stifling kitchen; the black monster of a cookstove. Even though Milo carried wood and water for her, it was still a tough job. He sighed and stretched out, pillowing his head on his arms. And it didn't look as though the power lines would be repaired today.

Rowan stood up and stretched her cramped legs, wincing at the pain. She started back toward the path with her half-filled bucket of strawberries, intending to walk right by Neal. But a gentle snore stopped her in midstep.

"Neal?" He didn't stir and she approached hesitantly. "Neal?" she repeated. She dropped down on her knees beside him. *So the boss is vulnerable after all,* she thought. Her green eyes darkened as they studied his bronzed face, the craggy roughness softened now in sleep. Funny, she had never noticed how long and dark his lashes were.

A fitful breeze lifted a lock of the white hair and left it casually on his forehead, giving an air of innocence to the strong face. How deceiving looks could be, she thought derisively as her gaze wandered over the supine body, lingering on the tanned, muscular shoulders exposed by the knit tank top and following the denim-clad length of the powerful legs to the dusty boots. She knew only too well how this indolent posture belied the ruthlessly persistent man.

She started to rise and escape to the house while he slept, then sank down again near him, caught up in mindless lethargy by the peace and quiet that even his presence couldn't disturb.

Sunlight flickered hypnotically through the tall oaks and her eye was caught by the lazy spirals of a golden butterfly about the filigreed blossoms of Queen Anne's lace in the meadow. She followed the hovering and fluttering of the delicate wings until her eyelids drooped and she blinked them wide again, focusing on the grazing mare instead.

She glanced at Neal. He hadn't stirred, the steady rise and fall of his chest attesting to his deep sleep. Unconsciously she breathed to his rhythm as she watched him, her eyelids drooping again until she, too, lay back, eyes closed. A smile played across her lips, soft now with sleep, her earlier hostility forgotten.

Neal awoke gradually, hovering between sleep and wakefulness and loath to relinquish the pleasant floating. *Rowan!* The thought of her pulled him back into full consciousness.

He had followed her to the meadow. He raised up on one elbow and saw the chestnut mare still cropping contentedly where he had tethered her, so he couldn't have been asleep long—just long enough for Rowan to slip away apparently.

He sat up with a groan and flexed his arms, the corded muscles working as they stretched and relaxed. He squinted as his eyes followed the westering sun and he rose with alacrity. He still had plenty to do today.

He paled beneath his ruddy tan as he stood up and saw the still form curled in the tall grass. What was wrong? He smiled a crooked little smile as he realized she was asleep, one work-worn little hand still holding the handle of the half-filled berry bucket.

His eyes caressed her tanned face, lingering on the soft berry-reddened lips parted so slightly in limp surrender to the deep slumber that claimed her and noting that the fine crease between the green eyes was scarcely noticeable. His calloused hand went out to push back the damp tendrils on her forehead, but drew back before he touched her. She looked so peaceful, he hated to wake her. But he had to get back and he couldn't leave her here.

He looked out over the meadow and noted the absolute stillness. Even the birds and buzzing insects were silent in the somnolent heat. Neal looked back down at Rowan, his gray eyes soft and a little sad. How he wished she could leave demons behind and always be this peaceful! He sighed and bent over her.

"Rowan?" She stirred, turning onto her back with a breathy sigh.

"Little one?" He kissed the tip of her sunburned nose.

"We have to go back, Row." He caught her hand as she reached up to brush away the annoying tickle of his mustache.

He released her hand as she struggled sleepily and she stretched sensuously with little murmurs of awakening.

"Mmmm. What-a-a-t?"

His eyes roamed over her slender form, captivated by the catlike grace of her movements as she struggled to awaken. "I said," and his fingers were firm on her chin as he turned her face to him, "we have to go back to the house now."

She arched her back and sighed. "Now?"

His heart ached to say, "Not now, not for a long while!" but he forced his lips to say, "Now, Rowan." He stood, tall and powerful beside her, and reached down to grasp her hands and pull her up. His arm circled her waist to steady her. He felt her stiffen and let his arm fall as she moved away.

The look in her eyes told him she was still puzzled.

"You fell asleep," he explained with a smile.

"*I* fell asleep?" She looked up at him in disbelief. "*You* were the one who fell asleep." That much she remembered.

"Me?" he teased, his eyes sparkling with mischief as he saw her confusion. "I couldn't sleep out here."

"Oh, no?" She was looking around, searching the tall grass. "There!" she crowed triumphantly as she pointed to the matted grass. "Right there is where you were sleeping!" she announced smugly.

He pretended to study the spot. "Mmmm, you may be right, Rowan." His lips twitched as he looked at the spot where he had found her asleep and then back again. He looked at her speculatively. He swallowed a chuckle at the look of confusion that passed over her face, to be followed by a deep frown between her brows.

Her eyes were flashing green crystals as she faced him. "That's right, Neal," she said emphatically as she drew herself up to her full height. "You were there." Her sweeping gesture indicated the space between. "And I was over here."

"And never the twain shall meet," he muttered as he followed the movement of her hands.

"Pardon me?"

"I said you were absolutely right," he said blandly.

Her chin went up and her eyes narrowed as she looked at him suspiciously. She stifled the retort that rose to her lips and turned toward the path. "I have to get to the house."

Neal grinned at the stiff set of her back as she marched away and followed her with long strides. "Yes, I do, too."

The mare whinnied and pawed the ground at their approach. "Star is ready to go back, too, aren't you, girl?" He loosed the reins from the low limb as he quieted the mare, then led her toward the path. "Come on, Rowan, climb on," he invited, as he maneuvered the mare to block the path.

She pushed her damp hair back from her forehead and

looked at him in exasperation. "Please move your horse." She stumbled back as Star nuzzled her shoulder.

"See, Star wants you to ride," he said lightly. "Besides," he shaded his eyes with his hand and found the sun, "it's later than I thought and this way is quicker. And cooler," he added as she dabbed at her upper lip.

She sighed. He was right. It was quicker. And cooler. And the sooner she got back to the house she would be rid of him, at least until dinner. She moved to Star's side to place her foot in the stirrup.

"Here, Rowan, let me." Before she could protest, his broad hands spanned her waist and easily lifted her to the saddle.

"Thank you," she managed to say coolly.

"My pleasure," he said and swung up easily to settle behind her.

Her heart set up a mad thudding as his arms went around her to hold the reins loosely in front of her. She swallowed hard and closed her eyes. *Hold on, Rowan. In a matter of minutes you'll be at the house,* she told herself as he turned Star onto the path.

Her eyes flew open. "Wait! Wait, Neal!" She pushed his arms aside and slid from the horse, landing in a tumble in the soft grass.

Neal leaped from the horse in consternation. "What is it, Rowan?" he called as she picked herself up and ran back to the meadow.

"My berries! I can't leave my strawberries!"

He stopped abruptly and his shoulders shook with laughter and relief.

She came back to him jauntily swinging the berry

bucket, a triumphant flush on her pert face. She set the berry bucket on the ground and lifted one leg to the stirrup.

"Here, let me help." He was behind her and again she was lifted to the saddle.

"And the berry bucket, please."

He handed it to her and fit one booted foot in the stirrup, then paused. "You're sure you're not forgetting anything else?" he taunted, a smile in his voice.

"I'm sure," she said calmly as he swung up behind her. She would refuse to let his nearness upset her this time, she told herself as his browned forearms went around her and his hands holding the reins rested easily on the pommel.

Star carried them quickly along the winding path, intent on reaching the barn. Neal gave her her head, although he was tempted to slow her down and prolong the ride. He resisted the urge to tighten his arms around Rowan, noting with some chagrin how stiffly she sat away from him. Still, this was as close to her as he was likely to get. He looked down at the soft brown hair blowing freely in the breeze and across her shoulder at the small hands clasped firmly on the handle of the berry bucket. The wide gold band on her finger winked back at him and he gave an involuntary jerk on the reins, earning a reproachful look from Star.

"Something wrong?"

"No, of course not." His annoyance with himself—and with her—crept involuntarily into his voice. They emerged from the woods and he turned Star toward the house. "Good, there's Jan."

Rowan saw Jan waiting on the porch, Boots cradled in her good arm. "It's about time, you two," she called. If she was surprised to see them return together, she gave no sign.

Rowan clambered awkwardly down from the mare, still clutching the bucket, before Neal could dismount to help her down.

"Rowan?"

"Yes?" She looked up at him impatiently.

"Don't go wandering off alone again." His eyes glittered like silver as he looked down at her.

"What was that all about?" Jan had hobbled to the edge of the porch and was looking at her anxiously.

Rowan bent down and scooped up Boots. "Nothing, Jan. Nothing at all."

chapter
8

IN THE MUGGY HEAT OF THE AFTERNOON, Rowan pushed one of the chaise lounges from the patio into the shade of a giant oak and settled down for the afternoon with a paperback and a tall, frosty lemonade.

Neal had taken Jan into town to the doctor and Milo and Slim had gone along, ready for a break from the endless cleaning up in the sweltering heat. She had turned down the invitation to tag along, preferring the prospect of a quiet afternoon alone.

She flexed her bare feet and stretched luxuriously, easing the kink in her back. The breeze was blissfully cool after the heat of the summer kitchen. She could well understand the country folks cooking in the summer kitchen to keep the heat of the woodstove out of the living quarters.

She leaned back and closed her eyes, letting the silence flow over her. Gradually she became aware of the drone of a wasp nearby, then a chattering blue jay's scolding from a limb above her head, then a distinct scurrying in the tree.

Bits of bark and leaves began to sift down, and stabbing shafts of sunlight filtered through the dense foliage. Shading her eyes with one hand to peer above her, she saw a pair of young squirrels scampering along a slender limb, edging closer as she sat perfectly still. A cardinal, blood-red in the shimmering heat, came into her line of vision, turning his head curiously to view the intruder to his domain.

A timid young cottontail warily paused for a drink from one of the puddles still dimpling the low places in the lawn. Boots, after making his way majestically toward her, paused beside her chair and deigned to jump into her lap where he settled his bulk comfortably against her. Her hand automatically reached out to scratch behind his ears and his fluid muscles rippled in delight at the attention. A wayward breeze stirred and she caught the heady scent of honeysuckle mingled with the rich, earthy smell of wet leaves and wildflowers.

Philip and Robbie would have so loved this place. The great globe of sun seemed to dim, and determinedly she picked up her book and turned to the first page. After reading only a few paragraphs, she let the book drop idly in her lap.

Her despair was replaced by a heavy-limbed lethargy, draining her of motivation. Even her eyelids were weighted, too heavy to stay open. The book slipped to the grass as she gave in to an overwhelming fatigue.

When she awakened, the sun was a crimson orb hovering on the horizon. Her hair was in damp strings, and she felt hot and sticky all over. What she wouldn't give for a shower! But the plumbing was still unrepaired.

The next best thing, she decided, would be a swim in the river. She quickly went up to her room and changed into her bathing suit, then propped a note on Jan's table before following the path to the river below.

She gasped as the water met her sunburned shoulders, then gave herself over to the cooling stream as she drifted languidly, for once her mind a welcome blank. She lowered the dark crescents of her eyelashes and floated weightlessly.

Some sixth sense alerted her and she opened her eyes to see Neal on the bank. Unaware of her presence, he stripped off his jeans and stood poised on the riverbank, his powerful body clad in swimming trunks. He dived into the water in one fluid motion

She lost sight of him until he suddenly surfaced near her. Then she heard his quick intake of breath at the sight of her. He smoothed back his wet hair and wiped the water from his eyes.

"Sorry. We just got back. I didn't know you were here."

"I was just leaving," she said laconically.

"No need to leave," he said curtly. With powerful strokes he moved smoothly down the river.

Annoyed at the interruption of her reverie and stung by his abruptness, she swam to shore. She hadn't planned so short a swim, but she probably should go back to the lodge and find out what Jan's doctor had had to say. As she waded in the shallow water, Slim came into view. A quick glance down the river told her that Neal was looking their way.

"Slim!" she called out impulsively. She'd give Neal something to look at. He turned, and she beckoned him over. *What will I say to him?*

"Sure hot today," he said. *So, he could talk! For the tight-lipped cowboy this was major conversation,* Rowan thought.

A surreptitious glance confirmed that Neal was still watching them. "I've been meaning to ask you, Slim . . ." *what had she been meaning to ask him?*

He looked at her curiously. "Ma'am?"

"About Toby." *Where had that come from?* "What does he do here?"

"Do? Toby's just a pet. He don't do much of anything. Besides, he's getting old."

"Well, I was thinking . . . you remember little Stevie Blake?"

A nod affirmed that he did.

"He was *such* a cutie. And a real cowboy in that red hat! I was wondering, if he and his family should come back, if he could ride Toby. If someone was with him of course. I won't be here, but surely somebody . . ." Aware her conversation was running to ramblings, she paused. *Why won't he say something?*

But he didn't open his mouth, just continued to eye her curiously. *He must think I'm crazy!*

"Did you ever try to teach a child to ride, Slim? I'll bet you'd be good at it. You seem so patient with the animals . . ." *and he sure wouldn't scare them off with words.*

"Yes'm, I did. My little sister . . ."

"You have a sister? How nice! I was an only child myself," she chattered on inanely.

"Ma'am, I don't want to be short with you, but I've got work to do. Boss don't pay me to talk."

No, you'd be a poor man if he did!

But before Slim could make a move to depart . . .

"Boss?" The call rang out over the water.

Rowan turned to see Milo on the bank. He cupped his hands to his mouth again and called. "Boss, the power men are here and need you at the house."

"Here, Milo," Neal called as he moved from the shadows

along the bank. He swam toward Rowan and Slim with long, sure strokes, slowing as he came abreast. "I thought you wanted to be alone, Rowan." He turned to Slim. "You come on with me!"

Neither man bade Rowan a farewell as Neal joined Slim on the bank. She watched their departure, then turned and swam aimlessly downstream until exhaustion and the lengthening shadows forced her to turn back.

Depression settled over her like a cloud as she wrapped the towel around her. What in the world had come over her? Slim must think she was an idiot! And Neal ... Wearily she climbed the steep steps.

Boots met her at the top of the steps but no one else was in sight as she walked back to the lodge. With bowed head she plodded past the damaged cabins, oblivious to the work still to be done. She ignored Boots's overtures, absently brushing him aside as he frisked about her ankles.

He sat back on his haunches and glared at her with hot yellow eyes as she trudged on past him. As if making one last bid for her attention he leaped through the air, planting himself firmly in her path with a sibilant hiss.

Rowan stopped short, shaken from her self-loathing thoughts by the aggressive stance of the cat. She looked in amazement at the arched back and laid-back ears, taken aback by the blaze in the vigilant feline eyes.

"Boots?" she said tentatively.

The wary look in the yellow eyes disappeared at her soft question and the taut muscles relaxed as she knelt beside him.

"Bootsie? What is it, boy?" Her slender fingers caressed the length of the furry body, gently kneading the firm muscles of the powerful animal.

"Just want some attention? Is that it, boy?" Her fingers continued their massage of the compact body and Boots arched into her stroking fingers with a throaty purr. The yellow eyes closed and he rumbled in satisfaction at her ministrations.

"That's it, Boots," she told him. "I have to get out of this wet suit." She didn't know where the men were, but she wanted to get to her room. She rose and Boots opened his eyes with a disappointed look up at her.

"Sorry, boy." She bent down to give him a final pat but he avoided her touch and stalked off without a backward glance.

She had to chuckle at his almost human air and went softly up the steps. She let herself in quietly and tiptoed past Jan asleep on the couch.

Back in her room, she peeled off the wet bathing suit and slipped on a cool cotton robe. As she toweled her hair dry she stared at the stranger in the mirror.

Dear God, what is happening to me? She flushed with shame at the thought of her behavior in the river—how silly to think her actions would affect Neal one way or the other. Slim had been merely a chance instrument, and she had used him. But for what purpose? What would he think? And Neal! What did she *want* him to think? In her distress, she was unaware she had called upon the God she had forsaken.

She stared at the apparition in the mirror as she relived the scene. She paced the confines of her room, catching distorted glimpses of herself in the wavy glass. Damp Medusa-like coils framed her white face and her eyes were wide in dark sockets. Her mouth was dry and she felt quite ill. Never had she felt so foolish and less like an enchantress.

She was overcome by a bone-weary exhaustion, each limb a dead weight as she moved to the bed. Maybe she could leave in the early morning hours, before she had to face Neal. They would manage somehow if she wasn't here ... but for now, she had to sleep.

She slept fitfully, dreaming that she was back in the river swimming in ever-widening circles that led nowhere and had no end. She awoke unrefreshed and lay staring at the ceiling as the purple twilight stole from the hills and slipped into the room.

The low, mournful notes of a bird outside her window caught her attention. Again the quivering song sounded as she slowly sat up. She held her head in her hands as the call repeated, a solitary sound that seemed totally appropriate.

Making a supreme effort, she got up and forced herself to dress. She could come up later and pack, but now she would go down to see if Jan had awakened.

Jan turned from the television set as Rowan came into the room. "Look, Row, the power is back on ..." Her voice trailed away as she looked in consternation at her friend. "Row, are you all right? You look terrible!"

Rowan folded one leg beneath her and sat back in an easy chair. "It's just the heat." She still felt too foolish to confide in Jan. "Are *you* all right? What did the doctor say?" She changed the subject as smoothly as she could.

"Tomorrow I can hobble about a bit more. How about that?"

"That's great! But so soon?"

"Soon? It seems like forever ... and I still have a long way to go." She eyed the heavy leg cast with distaste.

"I know it seems that way, but it won't be as long as it has been," she commiserated somewhat illogically, she realized. "Anyway, I wanted to ask you something," she again attempted to divert the course of the conversation. "I heard a bird outside my window making the strangest sound. A really melancholy call."

"Yes, I heard it, too. That's a rain crow," she exclaimed. "When it's this hot and humid, they call for rain."

"A bird calls for rain?" Rowan raised an eyebrow. "Does it really rain then?"

"Oh, yes, it rains," Jan assured her. "I suspect, though, it would rain whether the crow called or not, don't you?"

"I suppose so." She really didn't care. It was so comfortable here and she was still so tired.

"Neal, look at her. She's worn to a frazzle!"

Neal was standing motionless in the doorway, a peculiar expression on his face as he looked down at her.

"She needs a rest. Neal, why don't you take her to St. Louis with you tomorrow?"

Neal was curiously silent at breakfast the next morning, letting them argue over whether Rowan would accompany him. Rowan couldn't imagine anything she'd like less than a day in his company.

"Jan, I don't *want* to go to St. Louis! I don't *need* to go to St. Louis!" She got up to get the coffeepot. "If I go anywhere, it will be home." She filled Jan's cup with the steaming brew.

"No more for me, thanks," said Neal, as he pushed his chair back. "I'm going over to the stable, then I'll be leaving. Say, about nine."

"She'll be ready," said Jan, with a fierce look at Rowan as Neal left the kitchen.

"I *won't* be ready, Jan, and that's final." She set her cup down with a decisive click.

"Look, Row, I know you're not keen on Neal's company, but humor me," Jan said earnestly. "I refuse to let you go home looking like we worked you to death! Besides," she added impishly as she saw the obstinate look cross Rowan's face, "you wouldn't refuse an invalid, would you?"

"Invalid? Ha!" Rowan retorted, knowing she was fighting a losing battle. "Anyway, Jan, you can't stay alone yet. Your arm is still in the cast and your leg . . ."

"I can hobble around for what I need. Boots and I won't miss you two at all, will we, Bootsie?" She scooped up the furry feline with her good hand and cradled him in her arms.

It seemed to be decided, Rowan finally admitted, resigning herself to the trip. And at least she wouldn't have to face both Neal *and* Slim. If the subject came up, she would just refuse to discuss her folly.

She also had to admit she felt better in spite of herself after she got dressed. How many weeks now since she had worn nylons? Or nail polish? She had given herself a quick manicure of sorts and her hands didn't look too bad. The simple green shirtwaist with the wide belt was one of her favorites and she knew it nipped in her waist becomingly.

She didn't notice the twitch of Neal's lips as she seated herself well over on the passenger's side of the front seat. He still was unsure of the advisability of this trip, but he couldn't deny the idea of having Rowan to himself all day still had some appeal. He would have to be careful of his conversation, though. He would say nothing to antagonize her today.

Neal, too, had exchanged his usual working garb for a suit and tie. Covertly, Rowan observed the fit of the well-cut summer suit on his muscular body. The snow-white mane added to his distinguished appearance and was a startling frame for the deeply tanned face.

His white teeth flashed in a smile below the well-groomed mustache. "Ready?"

The twisting miles to the interstate highway passed quickly. Rowan could see little damage from the tornado as they passed the snug homesteads, only an occasional raw gash on a tree where a limb had been torn away.

"I don't know if you can see it from here," Neal was pointing to the left, "but that was Riddle's barn."

All she could see was a steep wood pile some distance away. "Where?"

"There. That pile of boards was one of the biggest dairy barns in the area."

She was silent, trying to picture a barn built from the wood piled like jackstraws.

"We were lucky, Rowan," he said soberly. "South of here, whole towns were leveled and lives lost. For some reason we were spared." He glanced at her. "The funnel veered away from Ten Oaks just a half-mile down the road."

She grimaced. God's grace, again, no doubt. She turned away and bit her tongue. She didn't want to get into a discussion about *that*.

I can almost understand Jan's love affair with the Ozark

Mountains, she mused as the car rolled along. The reddish gravel roads wound past small farms snuggled at the base of steep tree-covered hills, just visible now as the morning mist melted from the hollows. Weathered fences marching to infinity enclosed rock-strewn pastures green with new grass where plump cattle munched contentedly, followed by awkward calves. An occasional tipsy windmill lazily pumped water into the trough beneath it.

Closer to the road, she noticed a variety of wildflowers and weeds, beautiful in their own way. Most of them she couldn't name, but a few she recognized. Queen Anne's lace she knew, with its showy umbrella-like clusters of delicate white; and milkweed with its hairy pale-green leaves. She turned to look back at a thick patch of purple beside the road.

"Wild asters."

"Pardon me?"

Neal turned briefly to her. "I said those were wild asters back there."

"Oh, very pretty." Her eyes glowed with a lively interest that charmed him.

"Later in the summer the black-eyed Susans will be all over the place and most of these banks beside the road will be covered with goldenrod. Look there—" he pointed ahead of them—"a whole patch of wild roses." He slowed the car as they passed the low bushes, delighted with her enthusiasm.

"Oh, Neal, they're lovely!" The only roses she was familiar with were the gaudy reds of hothouse flowers. These were much prettier in their natural setting. The pink of the single petals was as delicate as the inside of a sea shell. Yet Rowan knew they must be hardy to survive the inhospitable roadside. She had always admired survivors—like herself—although she had to admit she hadn't wanted to survive.

She shot a keen glance at Neal and had to smile to herself. Was this distinguished man with the strong profile and the large capable hands really discussing wildflowers? This was another facet she wouldn't have guessed of the Neal she knew so long ago. *Is this contentment, this satisfaction with small, everyday things, by someone of his sophistication and intellect part of the sorcery of these hills,* she wondered?

And, Jan, too. She had to envy her serenity—not a dullness or complacency, but apparently a true inner peace. She sighed. She was glad some people could live this way.

They left the country roads and were soon moving with the heavy traffic on the interstate highway that would carry them directly into the city.

Out of the corner of his eye Neal watched her. Her hands lay limply in her lap and he frowned as the golden band she wore glinted in the sunlight. He knew it had never left her finger since she had come to Ten Oaks.

chapter 9

"We're just outside St. Louis, Rowan. Do you have any special place you want to see? I thought I would leave you some place while I take care of my business and then meet you." His eyes brushed over her. "Does that sound all right?"

"Of course." She sat up straight and tried to pull herself together. She got out her compact and comb and made some minor repairs.

"My business is in West County, so you could go to the art museum, or maybe the zoo."

She ran the comb through her hair. "The art museum sounds fine." It would be cool and quiet there, with nothing to remind her of cookstoves, demolished buildings, or the river. Above all, the river. She felt her face flush up to the hairline.

But Neal hadn't made even one reference to what had happened there yesterday. What she expected him to say, she couldn't imagine, though she had expected a nasty crack or two. Obviously, he hadn't been bothered.

"This is Forest Park," he was saying. "The museum is at the top of Art Hill."

She looked around the park as he drove slowly up the winding road. Lovely old trees shaded picnic tables laden with bulging picnic baskets and brightly colored coolers waiting for families who strolled the pathways. Perspiring joggers passed them, skirting anything in their path without breaking pace.

"A busy place, isn't it?" observed Neal.

"Yes, it is. I didn't expect to see so many people so early."

"Well, they get here early, stake out a table, and stay for the day. Here we are."

He stopped before the broad steps and came around to open her door. "I'll be back in about, oh, an hour and a half. Is that long enough?"

She looked up at him, squinting in the bright sun. "I'm sure it is." Suddenly she didn't want to be left alone in the formidable stone building. She swallowed hard. "Where shall I meet you?"

"We'll meet right here." As if sensing her feelings, he lightly squeezed her shoulder. "You can't get lost here, Rowan. It isn't that big." He gave her an encouraging smile and moved to the car.

The forlorn little smile she gave him as he got into the car and drove away tore at his thudding heart.

She stood for a moment on the steps and looked across the parking lot at the statue of Saint Louis the Crusader, forever astride his horse, gazing into the distance. Finally she slowly climbed the steps to the glass doors.

She moved past the rusted hulk of the massive iron sculpture in the lobby to the information desk where she picked up a brochure describing the exhibits.

"H'm." A display of decorative porcelain. That sounded good. A photography exhibit. Maybe. "A Max Beckmann Retrospective, a collection of two hundred of the German artist's oils, watercolors, and prints," she read aloud. Now that sounded intriguing.

She followed the signs to the display and began a slow tour around the huge room. Few others were there and she was free to linger before any of the works that caught her fancy. The bold, intense colors and the odd characters in the eerie settings made her decidedly uncomfortable the longer she looked. She walked swiftly past the remainder of the paintings, barely glancing at the last few.

With a feeling of relief she found the porcelain display, where the sunlight caught the translucent colors of a Chinese bowl and the delicate tints of a German Meissen pitcher. With a muffled squeal of delight she spied a Chelsea Rose sugar bowl, a twin to the one that had always rested on the sideboard at her Grandmother Kane's so long ago. Her eyes misted a little as she lingered before the display.

The exquisite workmanship of a miniature snuffbox caught her eye and then a covered urn. It was all so lovely, she wished she knew more about the craft. She would look it up when she got home.

Looking down at the watch on her slim wrist, she saw with dismay that she would have to wander about a bit longer before Neal would come back.

She looked up to see his tall form striding toward her and an unconscious smile shaped her generous mouth. She was ridiculously glad to see him. Quickly she turned away to admire a squat pitcher, intently studying the intricate design.

"Rowan?"

"Oh, Neal." She didn't quite meet his eyes. "Aren't the porcelains lovely?"

"Yes, they are, Rowan." He grinned broadly. His heart was singing. He had seen that smile when she saw him coming and if she chose to be distant now, he could wait.

"Are you ready for lunch?" The corner of his mouth quirked as he looked down at her.

"I'll say!" Her lips curved in an eager smile. "As long as I don't have to cook it."

They sat quietly waiting for their order and Rowan found herself relaxing, hardly self-conscious at all with the man across the table. The warm Bavarian atmosphere in the low-ceilinged room, the flickering candles, the mellow music, all wrapped her in blissful peace. She sighed with pleasure.

"A little different from the summer kitchen?"

She smiled back at him. "Just a little."

They ate with amiable small talk, savoring each bite of the sauerbraten and noodles, the red cabbage, and the crusty rye rolls with sweet butter. The white-coated waiter brought coffee and they leaned back with mock groans.

"Dessert, miss?"

"Oh, I couldn't!"

"Sir?"

"Nothing for me, thank you. You're sure, Rowan? The strudel is superb."

"Please, Neal, don't even mention it." She looked ruefully across the table, flickering pinpoints of flame dancing in the green eyes.

He leaned toward her, his arms folded on the snow-white tablecloth. "What else would you like to do today, Rowan? We don't have to go back yet." In the dim light his eyes were gray velvet as he watched her.

"Just sit here, please." The ambiance of the lovely room, the background of muted conversation and low laughter, and the waiters padding softly about catering to every whim was heaven.

"Afraid the management might object. How about walking off some of this lunch at the zoo?"

"If I can get up and if you think we have time, I'd like that."

"We have plenty of time, Rowan." He wanted to stretch out this afternoon as long as possible.

"Good. May we see the monkey show?" she asked with a grin as they walked to the car.

Her childish plea was so captivating, he wanted to hug her. "Wouldn't miss it, Row," he assured her.

He threw his coat and tie into the back seat and rolled up his shirt sleeves, exposing deeply tanned forearms. "There! that's better." Rowan's smile, in answer to his own, made him feel free and foolishly boyish.

They drove back to Forest Park, taking a circuitous route to the zoo parking lot. He pointed out the Municipal Opera, renowned for its summer productions and slowed as they passed the glittering glass façade of the Jewel Box.

"We'll come back here to see the flower display if we have time," he promised.

He parked and they ambled companionably down the paths, pausing at whatever struck their fancy. They laughed with the crowd as the seals nimbly caught fish thrown by the attendants and marveled at the radiant colors of tropical birds. The reptile house drew shivers from Rowan and they moved on to Big Cat Country, where lions, tigers, and jaguars prowled.

As they strolled away, Rowan sniffed the air, "Mmmmm, I smell popcorn!"

"Want some?"

"Oh, Neal, I shouldn't eat anything after that lunch."

"Stay here." He darted to the refreshment stand nearby and returned carrying an overflowing box of buttery yellow popcorn.

His face creased into a wide smile. "Here, eat what you can."

She found it impossible not to smile back. "You'll have to help." She popped several warm morsels into her mouth. "Delicious! Here, try some."

He munched on a handful as they walked. "Let's go in here." They turned into the children's zoo, a miniature world of baby animals in a natural rock garden setting. Hand-reared, the small animals knew no fear of humans and nuzzled the children who lovingly petted them.

"Let's sit here for a minute." Neal was absorbed in watching the children and animals, absently reaching for a handful of popcorn now and then.

Rowan sat beside him, her sense of well-being slipping away as she watched the children. *Robbie would be about that size now,* she thought achingly as a tow-headed youngster patted a woolly lamb. The popcorn stuck in her throat and she swallowed painfully.

Everywhere she looked, toddlers were gleefully cuddling the baby animals. Ripples of laughter filled the air as a wobbly brown-and-white kid sucked greedily at the bottle held by one of the children.

"Mommy! Mommy, look!"

She turned automatically to answer. But that wasn't Robbie calling out to her. Robbie would never call to her, never need her ... The popcorn scattered in yellow profusion as Rowan leaped to her feet and ran from the enclosure. Tears blinded her as she ran down the path, almost colliding with several people who turned to watch the white-faced woman followed by a big man moving swiftly after her.

"Rowan! Rowan, stop a minute!" Neal caught up with her and firmly grasped her arm. "Here, this way." He led her to a secluded bench shielded from the main walkway by a stand of pines.

She fumbled for a tissue. "I'm sorry," she said, her voice thick with unshed tears. "I thought it was Robbie ..."

"It's all right, Rowan," he whispered. He pulled her to him, his hand cradling her head against his chest. "It's all right," he murmured, his lips against her hair.

She was turning the ring endlessly on her finger, shuddering as she choked back the sobs welling without end from the depths of her being.

"Rowan, listen to me." He laid a large hand over her left hand. "Look at me, Rowan," he ordered. At the firmness in his voice, she looked up. "It was thoughtless of me to take you where that many children were liable to be gathered. I just didn't think ... "

"No, it's not your fault! I just made a spectacle of myself," she corrected him. "But I couldn't seem to help it." A gulping sob escaped her and she buried her face in the comforting warmth of his chest.

His arms tightened about her as she fought for control.

"It's all right, Row, it's all right," he whispered. He held her quietly, patiently stroking her hair, hoping to gentle the torment wracking her fragile frame.

Why hadn't he stopped to think what the sight of the children would do to her? He let her go reluctantly as she pulled away and sat apart from him.

Finally she looked up at him, afraid of what she would see there. She had ruined a lovely afternoon by losing control and causing quite a commotion. Incredibly no censure or derision showed in the gray eyes that met hers— only warm concern and apology. And something else she refused to name.

He took her elbow and led her to the car without saying a word, but it was a comforting silence that she appreciated. He gave her arm a sympathetic squeeze, hurrying her just a little until they reached the sanctuary of the car. Gratefully she sank into her seat and leaned back with her eyes closed.

From time to time Neal glanced at her but she seemed to have herself under control although he caught her dabbing at her eyes with a tissue several times. He refrained from any comment, silently praying instead, *O Lord, give her an end to her pain, some relief for the heartache caused by my stupidity.* His grip on the steering tightened until his knuckles were white. He flexed his fingers to ease the strain and raised a prayer for himself, that somehow he would be able to help her.

"It's about time you two got back. Did you get to see the Arch, Row? Or the Old Cathedral?"

"No, Jan, I didn't." She was pale but composed, numb

after the long, silent ride. "I spent the time at the art museum."

"Of course. I should have guessed," Jan chuckled. "Any exciting exhibits?"

"Oh, so-so." Rowan leaned on the newel post. "If you'll excuse me, Jan, I think I'll go up to bed." She gave her a wan smile. "We'll talk in the morning, okay?"

Jan sat up in consternation. Neal caught her eye and unobtrusively shook his head. "Sure, Row. See you in the morning," she answered.

Rowan climbed the steps slowly, each one an effort. She let herself into her room and kicked off her shoes and fell on the bed without undressing.

The room was dark and the house quiet when she awakened. She lay still, savoring the silence. Gradually her ears became attuned to the night sounds and she heard the wind soughing in the branches outside her window and the sporadic creaks and groans of the old house.

Unbidden thoughts of the afternoon chased through her mind. It had all been so pleasant until they went to the Children's Zoo. *Stop thinking about it, Row! It's over and done with and you're back at the resort, safe and sound. Safe, anyway.*

She got up and padded about the room, pausing at the window to stare out at the moonlit night. She needed something to do, anything but to try to sleep again. She paced the limited space, from one wall to the other.

It was too warm in the room, and she felt as if the walls were closing in. She looked down at the wrinkled clothes that clung to her feverish body and shrugged them off with distaste, letting them fall in a heap on the floor. She slipped into a short cotton robe and tied the belt with shaking fingers, then slipped on the terry cloth slippers beside the bed. She had to get out of this room!

She tiptoed down the stairs and stealthily let herself out the back door. She greedily inhaled the rich scent of damp earth mingled with the fragrance of wildflowers and honeysuckle.

It was as light as day from the gibbous moon, its less than perfect orb casting a shimmering radiance over the yard. She left the patio and walked through the wet grass, the heavy dew saturating her slippers in a few moments. Hoary fingers of moonlight probed the dense leaves of the giant oaks, dappling the grass beneath in ever-changing patterns.

Rowan saw little of the beauty of the night and heard few of the night sounds. Instead, in spite of her resolve, a jumble of sights and sounds whirled in her thoughts— laughing children, small animals, the smell of popcorn. She hugged her arms to herself, wandering desperately, aimlessly, across the yard to escape her thoughts.

She found herself back at the patio, the irregular stones rough under her feet. She stumbled and caught herself. A whimper escaped her and tears welled in her eyes. With a muffled cry, she dropped into a deep canvas lounge chair, her whole being throbbing with the sound of children's laughter. Sobs rushed to overwhelm her, the dam of self-restraint bursting, allowing the pent-up passions release. *Philip, I need you!* she cried inside. *My little Robbie!*

But it was Neal's work-roughened hands she remembered stroking her hair, his husky voice reassuring her.

Neal stiffly climbed the the bluff from the river, utter weariness in each step. He was tired from pacing the river bank, worn out from the emotional turmoil of the afternoon. He had gained some measure of peace walking until he could hardly put one foot in front of the other, but his heart was still sore with regret for the afternoon. He blamed himself for being so thoughtless, for exposing Rowan to a painful situation. He should have known better! He jammed his hands in his pockets, a drawn-out sigh escaping him.

He deliberately focused his attention on the beautiful evening. He always enjoyed being out after dark listening to the furtive skitterings and scurryings of the nocturnal animals. The distinctive buzzing song of the locusts rose in chorus, and as he walked beneath the oaks he could still hear the deep "jug-o-rum, jug-o-rum" call of the bullfrogs below the bluffs.

He stopped on the path and looked toward the darkened lodge, seeking the blackened squares of window in Rowan's room. He hoped she was resting well. She had been pale and shaky when he brought her home, although she had put on a brave front for Jan. He ached with her pain. His hand went up to massage the taut corded muscles in his neck. If only he could do something.

He moved on, reluctant to go in, and then stopped short as an alien note intruded among the familiar sounds, an all-too-human sound that caught at his heart. Swiftly he moved toward the patio, following the sounds he identified as weeping. He quickened his pace.

"Rowan?" he whispered as he knelt beside her chair. "Rowan, please stop," he begged.

She raised her tear-ravaged face to find him there, his hair a halo of pure silver in the moonlight. With an anguished wail, she leaned toward him, her arms raised in supplication.

In one fluid move, he rose, pulling her up with him. He held her tightly, pinning her against his chest, bending his head to shield her even more. She buried her face against him, burrowing into the strong column of his throat, seeking solace from the rugged bulk of him.

A low keening came from her, muffled against the sanctuary of his chest, an abandoned whimper that shook even his sturdy frame. Finally the sound dwindled away, replaced by hot, soundless tears that saturated his shirt.

"Cry it out, Rowan, cry it out," he murmured against her hair. His hands rubbed in soothing circles over her back, lingering on the delicate protrusions of her shoulder blades. *So much bitterness, so many tears, in such a small body.* Suddenly he hugged her fiercely to him, as if by sheer physical force he could end her suffering.

She was limp against him, soft shudders replacing the sobs, her grief spent. Still his work-roughened hands moved in sweeping circles across her back. *Weep on, beloved, weep till sorrow's end.* The fragment of the long-forgotten poem came to him as he held her. If only her sorrow could end.

Reluctantly, he released her as she pushed from the circle of his arms. He waited, his own legs unsteady as he watched her sink back into the chair.

Unshed tears glimmered in her eyes as she looked up at him. "Thank you," she breathed in a raspy whisper. Mercifully the night hid the blush of humiliation that stole over her.

He pulled a neatly folded handkerchief from his back pocket and knelt beside her. Gently he dabbed ineffectually at her red-rimmed eyes and tear-stained cheeks, causing a ghost of a smile to flit across her ashen face.

"Here. Let me." She took the handkerchief from him and wiped her face, pressing the cloth against her burning eyes.

"I'm afraid I've ruined your shirt." She sniffed and laid a small hand against the sodden material covering his chest.

He covered her hand with his own and held it against him. "It will dry, Rowan. No harm done." Her hand was warm against him. He longed to keep it there, but she withdrew her fingers one by one.

She studied her hands as she spoke. "Thank you, Neal." She raised her eyes to look at him through tears that hovered on spiked lashes. "I know that's inadequate, but I do thank you for your ... comfort." Her voice broke pathetically.

"No thanks is necessary, Rowan." He wanted so badly to hold her again but stilled the impulse lest he disturb the fragile calm.

"Yes, it is," she corrected him in a steadier voice now. "You've had to bear the brunt of my ... loss of ... control today." Her lips quivered.

He fought the impulse to still that quiver with his own lips and stood up instead. "Shall we go in?" he said hoarsely and held out his hand to her.

chapter
10

JAN LOOKED AT THEM WITH HALF-CLOSED EYES from her pillow on the couch. "Can't a body get any sleep around here?" she grumbled good-naturedly.

She looked from Neal to Rowan and sat up. "What's going on, anyway?" Neal was nearly as pale as Rowan. "Where have you two been?" she demanded.

"Just out in the yard, Jan," Rowan said stoutly. She turned away to hide the betraying quiver of her lips. Her fingers were white on the newel post.

"Oh, Row!" Jan heaved herself from the couch and stumped across the floor. She balanced awkwardly on her good leg while she put her uninjured arm around her smaller friend's shoulder. "Want to talk about it?" She flashed a disgusted look at Neal—surely Rowan's distress was his fault.

"No, thanks, Jan. Not now. Maybe tomorrow." She smiled tremulously across the room at Neal. "I think I can sleep now."

Puzzled, Jan glanced at Neal to see his mouth curved in a tender smile. She shrugged. "I'll see you in the morning, Row." She clumsily made her way back to the couch. "That is, if anybody can get any sleep around here," she muttered, "with all these mysterious comings and goings."

Rowan rejected the appealing thought of a hot bath as too much effort and fell into bed still wearing her robe. Drained, a hollow shell, she felt as if she could sleep for days.

Toward morning the nightmares began. She tossed uneasily as the insane laughter of children whirled around about her. The brilliant sunlight hurt her eyes as the children ran around her, their cries and laughter piercing the clear air. *Look, Mommy! Look, Mommy!*

Mommy, here I am. Mommy, Mommy . . . Robbie held out his arms to her and she ran to him, but he moved farther and farther away.

Robbie, don't go. I'm coming. She ran faster and faster but couldn't reach him. *Robbie, wait!*

Mommy! Mom-m-y-y . . .

He was gone. *No, Robbie, wait. Mommy's coming.* "Robbie!" Her cry shattered the stillness of the darkened room. She sat up in bed, drenched in perspiration. "Robbie, Robbie," she sobbed. She looked wildly around the room, completely disoriented.

"Sh-h, Rowan." Neal sat beside her on the bed. His arms went around her and he held her against him, rocking gently. "Are you awake, Rowan?" He turned her face up to him with firm fingers. "Are you awake?"

She fought through the cobwebs of terror-filled sleep and focused on his face, close above hers. "What happened?" she whispered. She stirred in his arms.

He held her firmly. "You had a nightmare, Rowan." He smoothed the damp hair back from her clammy face.

"Robbie?"

"Yes, you called for Robbie. Is that what the nightmare was about?"

"He called me, Neal, and I tried to reach him, but I couldn't! I ran and ran"—the words were strangled through the tears choking her—"and I couldn't get to him!"

"I know, I know," he crooned, knowing how empty his words were. "It was just a dream."

"You don't know! Nobody knows!" She glared at him with reproachful red-rimmed eyes. "Neal, I *saw* him and *heard* him!" Her lips clamped down on a sob. She moved from the circle of his arms and pushed down the light blanket.

She stood trembling beside the bed and grabbed a handful of tissues from the box on the bedside table. Furiously she blew her nose while tears coursed down her cheeks. She roughly wiped them away with the back of her hand and walked around him.

He watched her slowly circle the room and drop heavily into the rocking chair beside the window. She was crying quietly now, dabbing at her eyes with the sodden tissues.

"Row . . ."

"I'm all right, Neal," she whispered, turning her face away from him. "Please leave me alone now."

"*Now* what is going on up there?"

Startled, they looked at each other as Jan's voice carried into the room from the foot of the stairs.

Neal went to the top of the stairs. "It's all right, Jan. Rowan had a nightmare."

"Is she okay? Do you want me to come up?"

"Don't try to come up, Jan," Rowan called in as steady a voice as she could muster. "Please go on back to sleep."

"Sleep? Around here? With you two around?" They heard her clump back to bed and give an exaggerated sigh as she lay down.

Neal crossed the room to where Rowan still sat in the rocker. He gave her a lopsided grin as he ran a hand through his hair. "Jan's just put out because she's missing all the action."

"I know," she smiled weakly at him. "We have all the fun." Tears trembled on her lashes and she reached up to knead them away with her fist.

"Here. Let me." He grabbed a handful of tissues and knelt before her to wipe her eyes.

"Thank you," she sniffled. "I'm sorry, I can't seem to stop." The sobs swelled again in her throat and she cradled her head in her hands as the tears flowed between her fingers.

When the deluge was finally over, she sat with bowed head and studied her hands in her lap. Absently she twisted the ring on her finger until Neal's brown hand stilled her agitated one. She looked up at him and was taken aback at the understanding and compassion in his eyes.

He rose and pulled her up with gentle authority, his hands warm on the chilled flesh of her arms. She shivered and he pulled her close, warming her against the muscled firmness of his chest. She burrowed closer to him, her head seeking the hollow of his throat and her arms going around him, soaking up the gratifying heat that emanated from him.

Gradually the shivering stopped and she breathed

quietly, her soft sighs a delicious flutter on the hard column of his throat. His arms tightened about her slim form and he rested his chin in the tousled hair. For endless moments he held her, afraid of disturbing the fragile calm.

Finally she stirred and raised her head. Her long-lashed eyelids drooped as she gave him a vague smile, her mind benumbed and her body languorously warmed from his nearness.

"Come on, sleepyhead," he said in a husky whisper as he led her to the bed. "In you go."

She didn't protest as he settled her in bed, fluffing the pillow and pulling the light blanket to her chin. It felt so good to lie down and stretch out—to let Neal take care of her.

"Sleep well, little one," he murmured as he leaned over her. His calloused finger tenderly traced the lines of her cheekbone and across the still quivering lips to still them. "Sleep well." The brush of his mustache on her cheek was as delicate as the flutter of a butterfly wing.

"Will you stay here a few minutes?" she asked.

"As long as you need me, Rowan. As long as you need me."

Poised on the edge of slumber she watched him seat himself in the old wooden rocker, then bow his head into his hands. She drowsily realized he was praying. A faint smile touched with sadness at his foolish action curved her lips as she closed her eyes.

She awakened gently in the first light of dawn and lay quietly watching the day take shape, the gray squares of the window lightening even as she watched. Her eyes traveled around the room as the blurred edges of the furniture sharpened and the shadows faded from the corners.

Her eyes ended their journey at the wooden rocker. Scenes of the previous night drifted like wisps through her mind's eye. Faint color stained her pale cheeks as she felt again the encircling safety of Neal's arms and the steady beat of his heart beneath her cheek.

She tried to force her betraying emotions into order. Surely the tenderness she felt now was simply a reaction to the wracking experience of yesterday and the terror of last night. She would have turned to anyone and he happened to be there. Still, she knew his sympathy had been genuine and she was touched by his patience with her loss of control.

A blush like a shadow ran over her face as she remembered the heat of that solid frame, warming her own chilled body and soul and the viselike arms that had held her. How desperately she had clung to him in her despair!

Her eyes fell on the heavy gold band on her finger and quick tears stung her eyes. She folded her hands protectively under the blanket. Rowan clenched her jaw, her lips pressed thinly together to stifle the sobs that threatened, and fell into an exhausted, restless sleep.

She came back to reality too quickly, opening her eyes to a dazzling sun-filled room. She pressed both hands over her eyes to ward off the fiery fingers that probed at her red-rimmed eyes. As her eyes adjusted to the light, she lay staring pensively at the ceiling, errant memories of yesterday wandering through her mind.

Above all, the thoughts of Neal flowed through her, disquieting thoughts of his tenderness and concern. She was confused by her own response and a rosy glow suffused her whole body as she felt again his tight embrace.

Impatiently she pushed away such thoughts and concentrated on her immediate problem.

She wanted to go home. She couldn't take any more episodes like yesterday. Nor did she care to see Neal every day. If she left, he would find someone to help Jan. The first thing she would do today would be to tell Jan she was leaving.

"Well, I must say you look some better than Neal this morning," Jan greeted her with an appraising look. Her merry eyes clouded. "I'm really sorry I couldn't be with you last night, Row. How do you feel?"

"Better this morning, Jan. As for being with me, don't worry about it." She gave an artificial little laugh. "Your brother is quite a nurse."

"He's a rock, Row. One of a kind. And he really feels terrible about upsetting you yesterday."

"But it wasn't his fault, Jan! It was just something that happened. I just lost control."

"Anyway, how about some hot coffee? Milo left us a potful."

As the steaming brew warmed her inside and out, she mused over what Jan had said. She didn't blame Neal at all for yesterday or last night. Suddenly she wanted to tell him that she didn't hold him responsible.

"What is Neal doing today?" she asked as casually as she could.

Jan looked up from the morning paper. "Mmmm, I think he said something about working in the stable this morning. I told him he should go back to bed instead."

A pang of remorse shot through her. If he was tired, it was because of her.

"I think I'll get some fresh air, Jan."

"Oh, sure. Good idea." She was absorbed in the local news and gave Rowan a quick glance over the top of the paper.

It was a good idea, she found as she wandered out the back door. The cool air revived her and cleared some of the cobwebs from her mind. Maybe if she walked awhile, she could think clearly again. She stood for a moment on the back porch and breathed deeply as she looked around.

Mist still hovered over the valley, not yet burned off by the heat of the sun. Dew sparkled on the lawn and sprinkled diamonds over the cabin roofs. Before the sun rose much higher, the heat and humidity would again close in like a blanket, but for now, a revitalizing freshness greeted her.

With light steps, she left the porch and drifted toward the path to the stable. A few moments of brisk walk brought her to the edge of the stable yard.

Her heart beat faster and she stopped and looked toward the neat barn-red building. No one outside except Toby standing patiently under a shade tree in the pasture. If Neal was there, he must be working inside.

Her steps faltered as she started toward the building. Now that she was here, she couldn't imagine what she would say to him. Nor could she guess what his reaction would be.

She stopped and half-turned. Probably she should just let well enough alone and go back to her room and pack. She could write a neat, superficial note thanking him and Jan for their hospitality and let it go at that.

No, she argued with herself, he deserved more than that

after last night. She *did* appreciate his concern and it would nag at her until she told him so. If only she didn't have to face him to tell him!

Idiot! she scolded herself as she slowly moved to the door. *Just say thank you and leave,* that little inner voice urged. But somehow that seemed inadequate recompense for one who had held her together when she was falling apart from the inside out.

She stood in the doorway while her eyes adjusted to the dim light. She didn't see or hear Neal; even the stalls were empty.

Shrugging off her disappointment, she started down the passageway. At least she could see Toby for a minute. She jumped as Boots rubbed against her bare ankles, purring a welcome.

"Bootsie! Where have you been?" She scooped him up, hugging the solid body to her. "Pretty boy," she crooned. "You've been out running around, haven't you?"

His eyes gleamed like yellow glass as he raised his leonine head to look at her, assessing this strange human who held him. He settled comfortably against her as she scratched behind his ears and stroked his back, allowing her this privilege even though she talked foolishly.

"Poor Bootsie." She continued, "Were you scared in the storm? Did Bootsie hide from the bad old thunder?"

She sighed as he studied her face. "Boots, I wish I were a cat. You have only to worry about staying dry and well-fed. Someone to hold you and scratch your ears occasionally is all you need. Your fears are simple ones. Why can't mine be the same? Why am I afraid to think about the past? Why am I fearful of the present? And why can't I bring myself to even think about what the future may hold for me?"

"And why can't you talk to me like you talk to that cat?" came a voice from the hayloft. *Neal!*

Once more he had caught her in a foolish situation. He must think she was really an imbecile. First that inane episode with Slim, then falling completely apart at the zoo, and now, talking to a cat as if he could answer her. Worse yet, she had admitted to the cat what she had never been able to admit to herself—that she feared what the future might hold for her.

Slowly Neal descended the ladder, and crossed the barn floor to stand before her. "Answer me, Rowan. You've known me a lot longer than you've known Boots. Yet you can open up to him. Why not with me?"

She stood before him, shame and humiliation in her eyes. "Please, Neal, don't do this to me. Don't you know how embarrassed I am already?"

"Why? All you're doing is what everyone must eventually do—admitting that you fear the unknown. We all fear that; we all need help in dealing with it. God can help you come to terms with your fears, Rowan. And I can help you . . . if you'll let me."

"Neal, I'm already in debt to you. What must you think of me? I see myself as a helpless ninny. Everything I do continues to show me how weak I really am. I thought Stevie Blake had helped me to look at a child without remembering Robbie, and then that child at the zoo showed me I was wrong. Apparently I will never forget him—" she looked him directly in the eye—"or Philip."

"No one wants you to forget your child, or your husband. You are a woman who loves deeply, and you obviously were devoted to both of them. And you will always love them. Love doesn't die when someone is taken away from you—that much I know."

"How can you possibly know what I feel? You have never chosen to marry—to share your life, your whole being, with another. You have never had a child, who is a physical part of you, whom you love to a degree almost unbelievable. You've lived your life completely for yourself. And the only thing you know about love is what you might read on a valentine."

"I loved you, Rowan."

"Loved me? You didn't love me. You loved the idea of owning me—just one more possession to add to a long list. And you weren't willing to consider my feelings in the matter at all. Because I didn't fall down in worship at the feet of the charming Neal Conrad, you weren't willing to wait. What I wanted didn't matter at all."

Neal reached out a powerful arm to pull Rowan to him. His eyes pierced like steel shafts as he looked down at her.

Taking a deep, unsteady breath, Rowan attempted to speak. "Neal, I . . ."

"Never mind! Go on back to the house!"

She felt herself shriveling up at the distaste in his voice and eyes. She colored fiercely beneath his outraged gaze and moved toward the door.

He turned on his heel and strode swiftly from the stable without looking at Rowan. Her eyes blazed as he brushed past her without a glance, and she choked on the vehement protest caught in her throat.

She ran out the door and across the stableyard. She was gasping painfully when she slowed down on the path to the house and leaned weakly against a towering oak to catch her breath.

So much for the simple thank you she had planned. Why couldn't he just leave her alone? Yesterday had passed so smoothly, until she had seen the children. And he had been so solicitous last night.

Well, she just wouldn't let herself care what he thought of her. He obviously knew she had many failings. Why didn't he just forget about her and let her go on back to Chicago? Why must he continue to try to involve himself in her most intimate problems? Her thoughts spun incoherently in a turmoil of hurt and denial.

She forced herself to breathe normally again and her eyes idly followed a large black spider industriously spinning his web on the barbed stalks of a blackberry bush beside the path. Even as he spun, an unwary ant wandered into the gossamer threads and was instantly trapped.

As Rowan watched the ant's futile efforts to free himself, her lips curled in a grim smile. "Me, too, little ant. Caught in a web of my own making," she murmured. Why, oh, why, hadn't she taken the return flight home?

chapter 11

With an air of nonchalance she knew to be false, Rowan strolled into the keeping room where Jan was absorbed in a never-ending soap opera.

"How was your walk?" Jan inquired.

"Lovely," she fibbed, as she pretended great interest in the current crisis taking place on the screen. Right now she didn't want to discuss Neal with anyone.

Rowan's ostensible interest in the program soon palled and she roamed about the room studying the collectibles displayed on the shelves. She should pack, or she could go call the airlines right now.

"Do you want to talk now, Row, or after you crush that pitcher with your bare hands?"

"Wha-a-t? Oh, I'm sorry, Jan." She looked down at her fingers tensed fiercely about a beaked pitcher of blue spongeware and grimaced as she put it back on the hutch.

She looked at Jan with eyes dark with suppressed anger and hurt. "There's nothing to talk about, Jan, not now. Maybe later, okay?"

"Sure, Row. Anytime." Jan grinned as she lifted her plaster-encased leg. "I'm not going anywhere."

THIS BAND OF GOLD

The shrill jangle of the telephone startled them both. Jan answered and motioned Rowan back into the room. She spoke in monosyllables and Rowan smiled in amusement at the nonverbal messages of her eyebrows.

Jan put the phone down none too gently and turned to Rowan with a scowl. "When you see Neal—if you see Neal—would you tell him he is to call Reva?"

A curious pang pierced Rowan at Jan's request, but she agreed to carry the message. Thoughtfully, she left, her steps taking her automatically back toward the stable.

With some trepidation, she approached the open door. If Neal wasn't here, she would have to look elsewhere.

"Neal?" She entered the stable with tentative steps. "Neal, are you here?" she called more loudly this time.

She heard a movement in the hayloft and started toward the ladder when Neal appeared in the opening above her. He stood with legs outspread and powerful shoulders hunched, looming formidably above her.

"Yes, I'm here," he said savagely. Something she couldn't define mingled in the gruff words.

The time had come. She moved purposefully to the ladder. Nimbly she climbed up and peered over the edge.

Neal was at the far end of the hayloft standing near a small dusty window, his back to her. He didn't turn as she clambered up.

She bent down and brushed off the knees of her jeans, buying time. When she straightened up, he still hadn't moved. As she looked at him, righteous anger rushed to choke her at the sight of his stiff back, accusation in every line of his unyielding body.

"Neal?" Her voice rang out. "I would like to talk to you!"

Very slowly he turned, almost in slow motion, to face her. They stared at each other across a loud silence, only the dancing dust motes moving in the stifling air.

She controlled her voice and lowered her tone. "Neal, I need to say something."

"I can't imagine what you would *need* to say to me," he said with great irony. "I thought you had Boots to take care of those needs."

Her knees were trembling as she faced him and she sat down heavily on a bale of hay. "About this morning . . ."

"Ah, yes. This morning." He looked at her bleakly. "I owe you an apology."

"Oh?" she said coolly. "For what?"

His lips beneath the shadowing mustache twisted in a parody of a smile. "For interrupting your little session with Boots. I suppose I should have known that you prefer his company to mine. Apparently you prefer the company of anyone or anything over mine. I'm sorry I have forced myself on you, Rowan. I honestly thought I could help. But I see now I can't. You don't want to be helped; you don't want to get close enough to anyone—any human—to be obligated to share your feelings. You don't want to talk to me; you don't want to talk to Jan; you don't want to talk to God. And we all care about what happens to you. We all care a great deal."

She flushed guiltily. "I have to work through this myself."

"But you're not working through it. Just about the time Jan and I see a glimmer of hope, it all comes crashing down around us. I know you're uncomfortable here, but it isn't because of me or the tornado or Jan. It's because you are going to continue to be uncomfortable until you come to terms with your grief."

She regarded him coldly. "That is none of your business," she told him flatly. She lifted her chin and struggled to keep her voice even. "We were talking about this morning . . . why I came out here in the first place."

"And why did you come out here? To see Toby?" he asked sarcastically.

Her green eyes glittered as she looked up at him. "I came out here to see you," she said quietly.

He gave a mirthless laugh as he looked down at her with narrowed eyes. "You haven't sought me out before. What made today different?"

"I came to thank you for sitting with me last night." She twisted the ring on her finger as she spoke. "And to tell you not to feel it was your fault that I was upset."

His breathing had a ragged edge as he looked down at the slim finger weighted with the wedding ring, and her caressing fingers upon it. Her actions were like a flame to the tinder of his volatile emotions, fueled by his frustrations.

"Why should I feel it was my fault? You get upset with no help from me. How long are you going to clutch at those memories, Rowan? How long are they going to insulate you against any real feelings?" His eyes smoldered with banked fires. "Or is the insulation beginning to crack, Rowan?"

She flinched at his words and tried to swallow around the lump in her parched throat. "That's not fair, Neal," she protested in a strangled voice.

He groaned inwardly as the demon of frustration

gnawed at the very center of his being, stifling any of the gentleness or tenderness her stricken face evoked. He turned and walked away from her, the knuckles white on the brown hands clenched at his sides.

"Don't you know, Neal, that I haven't wanted to do any harm? Do you think I came here just to torment you? Don't you think I have any respect for your feelings?"

He pivoted to face her, his eyes raw with pain. "No, Rowan, I don't know if you do." His eyes burned into hers. "I have no idea what you think anymore. You won't let yourself feel, or love. Maybe that's how you've functioned. I don't know. But I do know nobody—not you, not me, not anybody—can live without love, whether it is the love of a husband, or a child, or a good friend. If you won't let me be anything more than a good friend to you, Rowan, I'll settle for that."

Mesmerized, her eyes followed his lips as the words poured out, words like bruising stones that hit her tender flesh. She winced as he impaled her with the steely glitter of his eyes, but she couldn't look away.

"Can't you answer me, Rowan? Or is it too close to the truth?"

"No, Neal. It isn't that way at all," she said in a suffocated whisper. She had caught the faint tremor in his voice and she looked up at him curiously. He looked drained and pale and quickly lowered his eyelids as she scrutinized his face.

She was shaking and sat down again on the hay bale, baffled, her mind a jumble of his charges. Philip, Robbie, Neal, Jan—they all seemed to be part of the terrible things

THIS BAND OF GOLD

he was saying, but none of it made any sense. She took a deep breath and stood up.

"Neal?" She looked at him candidly and spoke with a calm she was far from feeling. She held up a hand to still his interruption. "Just listen, please." Her words were slow and distinct. "I just want to say I came out here this morning to thank you for staying with me last night."

Her eyes slid over his still form as she turned gracefully and walked to the ladder. She swiveled back to him and met his fathomless eyes. "By the way," her brows arched derisively, "your girlfriend wants you to call her."

The sun was setting in the western sky when Neal wearily climbed the steps from the beach. He had walked for what seemed like hours, plunging through the woods like a madman after Rowan left the stable, circling the entire resort, up and down the steep hills, to finally end up on the beach where he had been sitting ever since.

He deeply regretted the bitter accusations he had flung at Rowan, and coming to grips with the fact that she was free to love—or not to love—anyone of her choice, without any explanation to him. And she had only wanted to thank him for his concern of the night before. Why couldn't he have just let her do that instead of asking for more from her. Would he never learn?

Lord, why am I so weak? You have infinite strength for your children to draw upon, and we continue to try to tap our own puny powers. If only I left this problem with you, instead of letting my temper take over. But, Lord, I still care for her. More than before, and in a way neither of us would have understood six years ago. If this is not to be, please give me the wisdom to see it, and the capability to accept it.

He knew Rowan misinterpreted his relationship with Reva. Why hadn't he just explained to her that Reva was the antithesis of everything he valued in a woman? But he had been acquainted with her a long time, and he knew she had needs, too. He continued to hope, since he became a Christian, that someday she would allow him to witness to her.

His lips, beneath the full mustache, twisted in a derogatory little smile. It was a good thing he managed his business better than he did his personal life, or he and Jan would be in the poorhouse by now.

Again he prayed, this time for Rowan, *Let her learn to live again, Lord.* For now, all he could do was pray. His anger had caused him to throw away his one opportunity to be a Christian witness and to listen when she had come to the stable to talk to him. It wasn't likely she would seek him out again.

Subdued, but with a measure of peace in his heart after his unburdening prayer, he squared his shoulders and walked toward the house.

Rowan toyed with the tea bag in her mug as she sat across the table from Jan, who had just finished a generous dinner.

"Rowan, even your leftovers are delicious," said Jan lightly as she leaned back.

Love and concern crowded Jan's brown eyes as she studied her friend across the table. "Row, I know I keep asking you, but are you still upset about yesterday?"

"No, not about yesterday. Well, some, I guess," she amended, "but right now I'm more upset about what just happened." An unnatural ruddiness stained the delicate planes of her face and emphasized the hollows of her cheeks as she met the curious eyes of her friend.

"What do you mean—just happened? Here?" Jan looked at her in surprise.

"Yes, here. Or, rather, in the stable, this morning. And especially just a little while ago."

Quelling the tremor in her voice, she briefly sketched the scenario and her futile attempt to make things right.

"Oh, Rowan, I'm so sorry. I was hoping this trip here would help you. And it just seems we've made things worse for you. Please forgive Neal. I know he can be hot-headed . . ."

"My sentiments exactly," Rowan quipped bleakly. "Jan, I can't believe Neal really thinks so little of me."

"I'm sure he doesn't, Row." She looked at her squarely. "Does it bother you that much?"

"Of course it bothers me! I don't want anyone to think . . ."

"Especially Neal?" Jan asked softly.

Rowan's mouth was distorted in a grim little smile as she studied the dregs in her cup. "Especially Neal," she admitted.

"Row, may I ask you something personal? You can tell me it's none of my business, but you are attracted to Neal, aren't you?" Jan asked hesitantly, watching the tell-tale tinge of pink that washed over Rowan's averted face.

"I don't know, Jan, what I feel. Mostly it seems to be anger, irritation, I don't know what else."

"Disloyalty? To Philip and Robbie?" Jan probed gently. Rowan looked at her directly with troubled green eyes. "Yes, Jan, disloyalty. And confusion, because there can never be anyone else in my life," she said with conviction.

"Oh, Row, please don't say that," Jan begged. "Life is good. And meant to be shared. Not necessarily with Neal, but with someone, if you'll just open your heart."

"My heart is full, Jan, and it has no room for anyone else," she said with finality as she rose to pour more hot water in her cup. "More?"

"No, thanks."

They both turned to the door as Neal came in. He crossed the kitchen to pour a cup of coffee.

"There's still some dinner hot in the oven."

"Not now, thanks, Jan." He looked at Rowan for a long moment, as if assessing her mood, then moved to the table and sat down.

Jan was silent, her expression thoughtful as she looked from one to the other. She struggled awkwardly to her feet, balancing on the burdensome cast.

"I think it's about time for my early evening nap." She smiled guilelessly at them. "Let's hope we *all* get more sleep tonight than we had last night!" She stumped off with a self-satisfied smile.

"Jan is so subtle," Neal commented dryly. He settled in his chair and reached for the sugar bowl. He carefully spooned the sugar into his cup and stirred it with great concentration.

Rowan watched him from beneath lowered lashes. She had felt a brief flare of anger when he came in, but that had quickly died to a bit of resentment that he could be so nonchalant after their earlier altercation. However, now that she saw that he looked worn and . . . beaten.

She quickly squashed the stirring of pity that rippled over her and tried vainly to revive her earlier anger and hurt. Oh, she was still hurt by his accusations, but it was more a dull ache now and she refused to care what he thought of her. Just talking to Jan even a little about it had helped. She allowed herself a faint smile, thinking of Jan's affection and concern.

She was aware that Neal had glanced at her sharply, no doubt puzzled by her mirth. Well, she didn't intend to enlighten him as to the source. She pushed her chair back and stood looking down at him.

"If you're sure you don't want to eat, I'll clear things away." She was pleased at how even and emotionless her voice was.

Neal, too, heard the lack of emotion in her voice. He had expected anger; in fact, he would *prefer* that she could at least muster up enough feeling about him to be angry. For some reason she was still speaking to him.

"No, I don't want anything to eat now. Rowan?"

"Yes?" She turned from the sink and eyed him calmly.

A claret stain crept over his deeply tanned face as he resolutely met her eyes. "Rowan, I have to ask your forgiveness for the things I said this morning. I want you to know that I realize I have no right to dictate the way you choose to live." He didn't take his eyes from her face.

She eyed him imperturbably. What did it matter what he believed about her now? She was leaving and he could keep his hills and trees and stables. She acknowledged his apology with a slight nod and turned back to the pots and pans.

Neal took a deep breath and leaned back in his chair, his long legs stretched out. He massaged the back of his neck with strong fingers as he watched her work at the sink, her own taut back and stiff neck speaking volumes. Nevertheless, he had come out of this better than he deserved, he thought humbly. He had been so sure Rowan would be gone by now, without a chance to talk to her again.

"Neal, I'll be leaving as soon as I can get a flight to Chicago," she said as if tuned in on his train of thought. "Jan can manage until you can get someone to do the heavier work." She kept her back to him as she industriously wiped off the countertop.

He straightened up in the chair and wiped the disappointment off his face as she turned around. "Let me know what time your plane leaves, so we can get there in plenty of time." He couldn't blame her for leaving but he knew in his heart it was the end of any hopes he had of winning her. He had taken care of that this morning, he thought bitterly, and had only himself to blame.

"Of course. As soon as I find out." She pushed the damp tendrils of hair back behind her ears and moved self-consciously to the doorway. "I'd better check on Jan."

He stood up while he desperately searched his mind for some reason to be with her this last evening. "Whew, it's so hot! How about one last swim?"

"Now?" She was startled by his request.

"Sure, why not? As soon as you check on Jan. We've got plenty of time before dark," he urged.

"Oh, I don't think . . ." she wavered. It did sound inviting, but she must be out of her mind to even consider going with him.

"Meet you at the beach," he said firmly as he saw her uncertainty, "in about twenty minutes."

chapter

12

HE WAS ALREADY IN THE WATER when she ran across the sliver of sand and plunged in. She swam to the willows downstream and back again while he lazily floated, content for the moment to have her near.

"It's too hot to swim that strenuously," he protested as she swam back near him.

"It's good for you," she said flippantly, at ease now that she was definitely going home tomorrow. She paddled in wide circles around him. "Come on, lazybones, get a move on," she teased.

"Lazy, is it? We'll see who's lazy," he challenged as he struck out in bold strokes upriver.

She watched his bronzed arms as their powerful strokes carried him far beyond her reach, and she idled along until he turned and came back.

"No fair," he accused laughingly. "You didn't even try."

"Well, in this case, retreat is the better part of valor, or however that phrase goes," she retorted. "You were too far ahead."

"Not too bad for a lazybones, huh?" His eyes glinted as he watched her.

"Not too bad," she conceded with a smile.

He was breathing hard and they floated inertly, watching the clouds in their fantastic patterns.

"Clouds are building up again," said Neal as he squinted in the sun. "Rain before morning."

"I heard the rain crow this morning."

"Did you? Just a bit of folklore, but uncannily accurate."

As of one accord, they reached the beach and waded ashore. Neal sank to the sand with a contented sigh. "It's much too nice here to go in just yet."

The setting sun cast a titian glow over them, making the scene a fantasy in red. Neal sat quietly watching Rowan, drinking in her presence, memorizing every line of her body. Her face was turned toward him, pillowed on her folded arms, dark lashes feathered on damp cheeks. Droplets of water still beaded her hair and body, ruby drops that shimmered with her every breath.

Her eyes flew open and every muscle tensed as he knelt beside her with his towel, but she didn't move away.

"You're still wet," he said as he tentatively began to dry her back. She flinched at his touch, but he steadily moved the towel over her shoulders, nudging wet tendrils of hair out of the way, drying her neck. She raised a shoulder and turned on her back to avoid the towel as he gently dried the pink convolutions of her small ear.

His eyes held hers for a long moment, as if plumbing the depths of her being. She looked back at him, his huge form silhouetted in the red blaze of the sun.

She could not look away as he slowly bent over her, closing her eyes only when his lips journeyed on their own across her heavy lids, down the flushed cheeks, claiming her tremulous lips at journey's end.

THIS BAND OF GOLD

Languidly she acknowledged his claim, relishing the tickling brush of his mustache as he savored her lips. Her hands moved of their own volition up his sinewy arms, slowly defining each muscle under the burnished skin with slim fingers.

His breathing was a discordant note and his vast chest heaved as she twined her slender fingers with his rough ones, while his breathy kisses covered the exquisite planes and hollows of her face. As from a great distance, she hazily realized his fingers had curved around the gold band on her left hand. Her euphoria vanished, swept away by his action.

"No, Neal, no." Her words were a smothered protest against her lips as she sought to shift her head to avoid his insistent mouth. His lips glided to her arched throat, resting on the throbbing beat there.

He raised his head in bewilderment as she rolled away and sat up in one fluid motion. The spell abruptly broken, he stared open-mouthed as she rocked back and forth in the sand, cradling her left hand, tears streaming down her face.

His hands clenched at his sides and his stomach knotted in remorse as he realized what he must have done. He vaguely remembered fingering her ring as he held her hand but it had been an unconscious gesture, wholly without any thought of removing it.

"Please, Rowan, I'm sorry. I didn't intend . . ."

"How could you, Neal?" she demanded furiously, her voice thick with tears, hurt and bewildered by his actions. "How could you be so underhanded and devious?"

Stunned by her accusations, he was speechless to defend

himself. Apparently she thought his kisses and caresses had been merely a scheme to remove the gold band. That gold band was the symbol of her self-pity! And yet, he hadn't given it another thought when for a few glorious moments she had banished the memories and clung to him.

"Believe me, Rowan, I had no thought of removing your ring," he began, when he found his tongue.

"You expect me to believe that?" she said scathingly. Tears hovered on her lashes as she glared at him. Her eyes never left his face as she rose and backed away.

She felt ill from the guilt that washed over her as she realized she had not thought of Philip and Robbie all day. This is what happened when she forgot, she castigated herself.

"Yes, I expect you to believe that!" Suddenly he realized she wasn't angry with him, but with herself for forgetting and surrendering to him. His voice softened and his eyes were tender. "Rowan, listen to me," he pleaded. "Loving again in no way diminishes your love for your husband and son. In fact, someone once said that the more one has loved before, the greater the second love can be." He spoke softly, calmly, sensitive to her internal struggle.

"Love?" She shook her head in denial. "No, no, no," she moaned. "No more love. You don't understand!"

"I do understand, Rowan. They're dead. Gone from this life!"

His words crashed about, bombarding her with pain. Her eyes were enormous and swollen with tears. "Why are you doing this to me, Neal?" She begged for an answer. "Why don't you leave me alone?"

"Why?" he said harshly and moved swiftly to stand

directly in front of her. "I'll tell you why. Because I want to see you smile," he rasped. "Hear you laugh! And above all, Rowan, see you live again!"

She sat with her head bowed to her knees, holding herself and rocking back and forth. "You don't understand," she repeated in a hoarse whisper.

"What I do understand, Rowan, is that you're consumed with self-pity! That whenever you want to avoid any confrontation, you fall back on your 'memories.'" He made the word revolting, searing her with his scorn. "How many times just since you've been here have we gone through these little scenes, these tearful little dramas, because I always seem to say or do the wrong thing?

"These last few weeks have been like living in one of those interminable soap operas of Jan's," he grated. "I'm trying to understand why you continue to saddle yourself with this indulgence, this refusal to face facts." He raked his fingers through the mane of white hair in utter frustration.

She stared up at him in disbelief, her eyes clouded in anguish, inarticulate in the face of his overpowering anger.

"There is something I *do* understand, though, Rowan," he continued as his blazing eyes raked her bloodless face. "And that is that they're dead!" he thundered, his voice echoing in the silence.

His voice, his words, flayed every inch of her being, leaving her raw and wounded. "Bu-but, he was my ba-a-by!" she wailed in agony, the words torn from her, strangled through the sobs lodged in her throat.

"My baby!" She was crying softly now, great, hot tears burning down her pale cheeks. "My little boy."

Her cries filled his ears until the pain he endured was as great as the torture he had inflicted. His anger turned to ashes, spilling from him in a rush, leaving him weak and shaken. "Rowan, please listen," he begged when he could speak.

The bottomless green eyes looked up at him, through him, suddenly frighteningly calm. "Never," she said.

His powerful shoulders sagged and the broad brown hands slowly unclenched as he turned wearily away. "It's no use," he murmured sadly. "I can't compete with ghosts."

A blindingly brilliant sunrise mocked her sluggish awakening and she quickly lowered her eyelids against the vibrant streaks of gold, magenta, and orange that assaulted her feverish eyes. Cautiously she opened her eyes again, noticing that she hadn't even closed the drapes in her bedroom last night.

She did recall leaving Ten Oaks and seeing the shining steel arch that guarded the Mississippi riverfront as the plane circled in takeoff, but the flight home and the taxi ride to her apartment were equally hazy in her mind.

She raised up on one elbow to look at the clock on the bedside table. It was just a little after seven and she knew it had been early afternoon of the day before when she had arrived, physically and emotionally exhausted, and had fallen immediately into bed. Well, she hadn't quite slept the clock around, but not far from it.

Nagging thoughts of her hasty departure picked at her and she burrowed down into the pillows as she thought of Jan's tearful but sympathetic good-by and the silent drive with Milo to the airport. The old man hadn't pried, but he obviously had realized something was wrong and had respected her silence. She smiled a little thinking about his clumsy but affectionate farewell. She would miss him. And Jan, of course.

What she wouldn't miss would be Neal and their tempestuous confrontations. Or his self-serving advice. She grew warm all over as she thought of their last encounter at the river. She still didn't understand how she could have so forgotten herself. And she certainly couldn't stay after that!

She shook her tousled head to banish the memories, pushed back the sheet and sat up. Her face softened as the smiling faces of Philip and Robbie beamed at her from their gold frame on the dresser. She smiled back. It was good to be home!

She stretched luxuriously and slipped into a short terry robe to pad barefoot through the apartment, composed of what originally had been two rooms of a graceful old Victorian house on Chicago's Near North Side. One sizable chamber was divided into a living/dining area with a small, efficient kitchen; the second made up her spacious bedroom and bath. The gracious ambiance imparted by the high ceilings, ornate light fixtures, and rich dark woodwork always gave her pleasure.

Rowan paused in the living room by the French doors that led to a pocket-sized patio, where riotous red and white geraniums flourished in clay pots. Their nodding heads welcomed her and she smiled briefly at them before continuing on to the kitchen.

She filled the teakettle and set it on the stove. A quick check of the refrigerator revealed little except a tub of margarine, a half loaf of frozen bread, and a dried-up nubbin of cheese. It looked like she would eat tea and toast until she shopped.

She turned down the burner under the teakettle to give her time to shower and went back to the bedroom, where she paused to efficiently smooth the rumpled bed before she went to the closet.

A sharp pang jolted her when she saw Philip's blue suit hanging behind her dresses and Robbie's small shoes on the top shelf. She had given away most of their possessions when she moved here, but couldn't bear to part with every last thing. Even as she stood there, compelling memories washed over her, but she reveled in them, finding comfort at the edge of grief. This was where she belonged!

A pair of blue cotton slacks and a white shirt would do for a summer day in Chicago and she laid them on the bed before she headed for the shower.

She closed her eyes and let the hot water beat over her, stinging pellets that made her skin tingle and pinken. Her fingers found the soap dish and the bar of apple blossom soap that Philip had always bought for her. She used the fragrant bar to lather herself slowly and sensuously in the deluge of steamy water. Vagrant thoughts of the last few weeks floated to mind, but she held them at bay.

Rowan reached for the deep-piled bath towel and dried herself vigorously, rubbing away those errant thoughts that appeared annoyingly to plague her. She was home now, safe and sound. And she intended to stay that way.

The teakettle had reached a slow boil by the time she got back to the kitchen and she made the tea strong, letting the teabag dangle in the cup an extra minute or two while the bread toasted. She slathered the golden margarine on the crisp toast and carried it to the table, sitting where she could look out the open back door into the tiny back yard, which was bordered on the alley by an old brick wall, the color faded to a soft rose shade.

She should call the office, she mused, but she would wait until Monday. She could have a whole weekend to herself. She would stock up on groceries and library books and not let anyone know she was back. She took a heartening swallow of hot tea and reached for a pad and pencil to make her grocery list.

Her phone was ringing as she fumbled with the key in the lock and finally pushed the door open. She dumped books and groceries on the table and reached for the phone.

"Oh, Jan!" she exclaimed. "I couldn't imagine who would be calling." Ridiculous tears moistened her eyes at the sound of Jan's voice. She could picture her on the couch with her cast propped up and lounging back with the phone.

"Just me, Row, wondering if you're all right."

"I'm fine, Jan. Just getting settled in with groceries and all. Are you managing all right?" She still had a lingering guilt about leaving Jan to fend for herself, although she was far from helpless.

"Yes," said Jan heartily. "Mae agreed to come back for three or four days a week, so we're managing . . ."

Her voice trailed away and goose bumps prickled up Rowan's spine. "You don't sound right, Jan. Is something the matter?" she asked warily.

"No," she answered too quickly and then sighed. "Yes, I think there is, Row, but I don't know for sure." She paused as if debating whether to continue.

"What is it, Jan?" Rowan prompted cautiously.

"It's just that . . . Neal's gone, Row. I don't know where!" she burst out. "He was here just after you left, but no one has seen him since."

"But he always tells you where he's going, doesn't he?"

"That's the whole thing, Row. He didn't say a word and that just isn't like him."

"Could you just have forgotten some appointment he had?"

"I'm sure there was nothing like that, Row. I even checked the calendar in his office."

"Well, Jan, I really have no ideas at all." Or care, she thought cynically.

"I know, Row. It's just that, well, frankly, I'm worried. He was so depressed after you left."

"Oh, Jan, surely you don't think . . . ?"

"I don't know what to think, Row. All I can do is wait, I guess."

Rowan hung up after a few more moments, a frown marring her smooth forehead. She was sure Jan was needlessly worried. She had no doubt that Neal would turn up when he got good and ready; he always had, no matter the worry he caused in the meantime.

She put away the groceries and looked at the books on the table. Her hard-won composure was disturbed and a restlessness had set in, making an evening with even her favorite author extremely unappealing. A trace of resentment goaded her, a distinct feeling of annoyance with Jan for disturbing her, which she knew was unfair. Resolutely she decided to call a friend and go out for dinner. She picked up the phone only to put it down again. She really didn't want to do that, either.

She paced the limited confines of the apartment. She didn't want to think about Neal, or where he might be. Oh, if only she could wipe out the last few weeks!

Finally she prepared the inevitable cup of tea and picked up the mystery that looked the most involved. Maybe getting involved in a good fictional murder or two would occupy her mind and blot out those nuisance thoughts that hovered around the fringes of her mind, ready to take over should she relax her vigilance.

The insistent ringing of the doorbell pulled her from the depths of the mystery novel, and she became aware that the outside was filled with soft blue twilight. She smoothed back her hair and switched on another lamp on her way to the door. She opened the door as far as the chain lock allowed and peered through the narrow opening.

Neal had never felt so foolish—or determined—as Rowan stared at him through the barely opened door. He hated the way she had fled Ten Oaks. And he hated himself for his part in her precipitous departure, realizing he had taken advantage of her vulnerability. He burned with shame when he thought about it. He had prayed and agonized over the decision to follow her to Chicago, and had felt led to explain his actions to her and ask for her forgiveness. He wouldn't blame her if she refused to let him in. He ran splayed fingers through his tousled hair.

In a state of shock at seeing him outside her living room, she automatically released the lock and stepped aside as he pushed open the door. Her breath caught in her throat as he strode past her. She was rooted to the spot as he turned to face her.

"I've prayed about this, Rowan, and felt I had to come." His voice was low and tired and seemed to come from a great distance.

With detachment she noticed the deep lines on his face from nose to mouth and the gray pallor beneath the bronzed skin. She was silent, unable to utter a sound. She eyed him warily as he continued.

"I guess it's my turn to be sure you understand my actions," he said wryly. "I can only hope you are more charitable than I was." He looked at her bleakly across the space between them and wearily rubbed a large hand over his stubbled chin. Her silence was disconcerting. Obviously she wasn't going to make this any easier.

"I know there can't be anything between us." He held up a hand to still her as a sound escaped her. "But if you ever need anything I want you to call me. Understand?"

She shook her head dumbly. Surely he hadn't come all the way to Chicago to tell her that!

She watched as he walked to the French doors and stood looking out at the twilit patio, his hands jammed in his pockets and his shirt stretched across his hunched shoulders.

"And, also, Rowan, to tell you my actions at the river grew—no matter what you think—out of love," he whispered. He turned to look at her, his eyes as softly gray as velvet, a barely discernible flame flickering in their depths. "Because I care, Rowan."

His words hung in the air between them. *No, don't say*

that! she wanted to cry. *Just go away!* But she was speechless, her heart pounding loudly in her ears, every nerve steeled against the onslaught of his words.

His eyes bored into her, compelling her by his very will to look at him. The interminable silence lengthened, stretched to the breaking point, before she raised her eyes, dark with pain and disbelief, to stare at him.

"Because, God help me, Rowan," his voice was a grating whisper in the silence, "I love you!"

Only when the latch clicked did she move, numbly slumping into a chair where she sat gazing blindly into the darkening patio.

Dusk had deepened to inky blackness before she stirred. Mechanically she rose and prepared for bed, not bothering to look at a clock, a curious emptiness about her as she brushed her hair and slipped into a soft cotton gown. The eyes that looked back at her from the mirror over the washbowl as she brushed her teeth belonged to a stranger, one who allowed only the most mundane of thoughts to enter her mind.

She collapsed into a fitful sleep and tossed and turned as his words pounded at her relentlessly. *Dead and gone! Dead and gone!* She dreamed of the river and the mountains, but all had a nightmarish quality as his words hung in a pall over the whole scene. And then the softer, even more devastating words—*I care ... I love ...*

She had never been a fanatical housekeeper but now she became a whirlwind of activity, cleaning the apartment from top to bottom, polishing and scouring until she fell asleep each night propped against the pillow with a book in her hands.

THIS BAND OF GOLD

Every cut-glass dish in the corner cabinet was washed and dried with a soft cloth until the faceted surfaces caught the light and became flashing rainbows about her. She cleaned and waxed the old oak floors and was rewarded with an almost crippling backache.

She attacked the kitchen with a vengeance, removing the contents from each cabinet, ruthlessly discarding carefully hoarded, but useless items. Cans, boxes, glassware and dishes stood in orderly precision, giving her a sense of control over her life, a feeling that had been sadly absent for a long time.

She didn't answer the phone, some sixth sense telling her Jan was trying to contact her. Right now she couldn't bear to talk to her, refueling the memories that plagued her in the dark hours before dawn. She could have handled nightmares better, she thought, but these annoyingly inevitable dreams of green spaces, wooded hills and fragrant wildflowers evoked a longing during her waking hours she found harder and harder to ignore.

This was where she belonged! If she just kept busy enough these ridiculous dreams and longings were bound to disappear. She had deliberately sought out all the things in the apartment that reminded her of Philip and Robbie, and the little treasures she had kept, all were very much in evidence.

Incredibly she realized this simply wasn't working! Their images were no longer so sharp nor her grief so overwhelming. In fact, she hadn't collapsed in tears even once since her return. Or was it that she had cried herself out at Ten Oaks, exhausting herself emotionally, leaving only a hollow shell, devoid of any feeling?

She walked through the apartment, touching her belongings with a loving hand, picking up the vase she and Philip had purchased on their honeymoon. Suddenly the squeaky clean rooms didn't please her and seemed to close in on her. She set the vase down harder than she intended and walked to the French doors where she looked out with jaded eyes.

The tiny back yard with its spindly tree was a joke and the pots of flowers on the patio were poor imitations of the profuse wildflowers in their natural habitat that abounded in the mountains.

What a mood she was in! She gave herself a mental shake. A brisk walk might help. And a hot meal. She had simply been alone in the apartment too long, subsisting on hot tea and canned tuna.

chapter
13

THE CHICAGO SUMMER DAY was perfection, with warm sunshine, cooled by a breeze ruffling the waters of Lake Michigan. She took a deep breath and threw back her head. A smile played over her lips as she walked briskly with a free and easy stride. But then, simply walking and window shopping, never tiring of the changing displays in the huge windows or the glimpses of the lake and its parklike shoreline, had always been favorite pastimes.

Her long absence from the city made her feel almost like a tourist. But in spite of her pleasure in the city, today the raucous horns of the traffic seemed louder and more annoying; the pall of the everpresent pollution, heavier. The plate-glass windows of the shops were hard and glaring, the displays less fascinating. Even the sidewalk seemed harder and more unyielding beneath her sandals.

That's what a few weeks in the country will do, she thought wryly. Disappointed, she followed the hurrying throngs, alone in the crowd.

But her mind strayed to the lush green Ozark hills with their tapestry of myriad greens as far as the eye could see, the delicate blooms along the path to the stable and the curving drive lined with the majestic oaks. The silver ribbon of the river . . .

Neal's voice ran rampant over her senses as she replayed the scene at the river over and over, hearing his cutting words begin to take on the ring of truth. He had brutally accused her of self-pity; was she really guilty as charged?

She walked faster and faster, the yellow blouse beginning to stick to her with perspiration. No, her overwhelming emotion was simply grief, which was natural, wasn't it?

She heard again the words that had painfully reopened her healing wounds, scathing in their accusations.

And then, she heard again his last weary words, so softly whispered to her in her apartment that last night he was there.

She was almost running now, back to the sanctuary of her apartment. She couldn't—wouldn't—learn to care for someone and run the risk of losing him again! She was oblivious to the horns that blared as she darted across the street on a yellow light.

She wandered about the apartment, alone again in the lovely cool silence with her pictures and memories. She couldn't settle down, though, beginning to pace with an agitation she was loath to analyze.

Like a pesky mosquito buzzing about her, Neal's declaration of love teased and refused to be banished. She realized he had been in her thoughts more than Philip, even more than Robbie, hovering just beneath her consciousness, waiting to surface. For the first time, her memories weren't much comfort. She wanted more than just memories!

Hardly aware of its happening, she found herself praying

in halting supplication for strength and guidance, praying to a God who was there, waiting. A God, she realized even in her anguish, who had not abandoned her, even when she would turn away.

Neal had been right, she thought, feeling strangely calm and rational. Philip and Robbie *were* gone. And all her denial of that fact wouldn't bring them back.

They were gone, but God was there! They were dead, but she was alive! And Neal had declared his love for her. Did she love him? She didn't know. She couldn't analyze that deeply yet. But neither could she deny she had some feeling for him.

She was suddenly filled with exultation. Her limbs were shaky and she felt she had run miles, but inside she felt strong and at peace, able to tackle this business of living. She made a wobbly journey across the carpet to stare at herself in the mirror.

"You have a lot of living to do, old girl," she told the reflection with the bright green eyes.

But now, more than anything in the world, she wanted to go back to Ten Oaks. And to Neal.

Rowan was inordinately disappointed to find the first plane seat available would be late the next night. She wanted to pack up and leave Chicago immediately. She was filled with the vibrancy of unleashed emotions too long held in check and needed to act on this new-found freedom.

She had lain awake most of the night waiting for the new day, savoring the memories of the last few weeks. *I* love you . . . I *love* you . . . I love *you*. Any way she said it made her feel warm and glowing all over.

Only the little niggling doubt of her own feelings for him cast a small shadow. She must see him; must resolve those doubts.

And now to have to wait all day and most of the evening before she could leave! She watched slim golden fingers of the rising sun probe the half-open slats of the window blinds, sliding in between to erase the gray shadows, playing across the sheet that covered her. She lowered feathery lashes to shut out the glare and tried to think rationally.

Finally she swung her legs over the edge of the bed and walked decisively to the closet. She would pack up her little red car and drive to the Ozarks herself! She had never driven that far alone, but she had no qualms that she could do it. Perhaps not in record time, but she would be there by early afternoon at the latest.

She made herself take the time for a quick, light breakfast, which she ate without tasting. She rinsed out the dishes and looked rather absently around the apartment, assuring herself that everything was in order.

It took only a few minutes to stow a few clothes still on hangers and her overnight case in the back seat. Thank goodness the gas gauge showed almost full. She wouldn't have to waste time at a service station.

Eager though she was to leave, she sat still for several moments and finally lowered her head to rest on her hands clenched about the steering wheel. Her fingers relaxed and she raised misty eyes to stare through the windshield while she turned on the key. She had one more thing to do before she headed for Ten Oaks.

Tranquility surrounded her as she guided the little sedan

along the meandering drive to the Hayley family plot deep within the cemetery. She spotted only one other car in the vast grounds as she drove through the shady tunnel created by the giant maples on either side.

She parked and walked up the gentle slope to the Hayley section as she had done so many times in the past three years, skirting the lichened headstones of Philip's forebears who rested there, until she came to the newest stones.

She knelt between the two mounds and her eyes traveled over the headstones, absently reading the names and dates chiseled forever in the stone. Her expression was pensive as she leaned over to pull a stray weed from the lush green ground cover she had planted and faithfully tended, then reached with a steady hand to straighten the floral arrangements which graced each grave.

Rowan sat back on her heels and looked out over the rows of headstones. For the first time she did not feel their presence and in her heart she acknowledged that Philip and Robbie were not here. Her face was calm with just a hint of sadness in the green eyes as she read again the words—just commemorations of their time on this earth, she finally admitted to herself.

Tears glistened in her eyes but her smile widened at the surge of peace through her whole being. *I know now where they are,* she exalted as she turned her face to the heavens. *And I know where God is, too!*

A torrent of tears streamed down her tanned cheeks as the sheer joy of her knowledge swept over her. *Thank you, Father; thank you.* She whispered the litany of praise and thanksgiving over and over, then raised her head and smiled a tremulous smile of bottomless peace. She gave a long sigh of contentment and stood up.

Once more her eyes lingered over the two mounds at her feet and in her heart she released that part of her life and turned to leave.

Before long she was out of that early morning migration of thousands of white- and blue-collar workers that regularly filled the city. She maintained a steady speed and the little car gobbled up the miles. She rolled the window down and let the warm brown tendrils of her hair blow wild and free. It was a euphoric feeling that brought a radiant glow to her delicate face.

The closer she came to her destination, the more doubts assailed her. What if Neal had changed his mind? She tried to smother the thought, but perhaps he really had already written her off as hopeless, as well he might.

Had she been too hasty, rushing pell-mell back to Ten Oaks with only a confused conception of her own feelings? And she hadn't even called Jan to tell her she was coming. She had been afraid Neal would answer and she hadn't felt she could talk to him over the phone. She should try to reach Jan, though.

She pulled in at the next rest stop and stiffly got out of the car. Her leg was cramped from driving too long and she limped painfully to the phone.

With trembling fingers, she dropped in the coins. She smoothed back her wind-blown hair impatiently as the interminable minutes passed, punctuated by the insistent ringing at the other end. *Oh, Jan, please be there,* she implored silently. *Please answer!*

"Hello."

"Oh, Jan, thank goodness!" Her knees were weak with relief.

"Row! I've been trying to get you! Where have you been?"

Rowan felt a warm glow steal over her at the concern in Jan's voice. "I've been at the apartment. It's a long story, Jan."

"But I've called and called!"

"I'm sorry. But, Jan, I need to ask a favor of you. Is it all right if I come back to Ten Oaks?" she finished breathlessly.

"Come back?" Rowan could hear the puzzled note in Jan's voice. "Of course it's all right, Row, but why?"

"I have to see Neal!" Rowan said jubilantly. "I have to talk to him."

"Oh, thank God!" Jan whispered. "Oh, Row, I'm so happy for you." She was laughing and crying. "When can you come?"

"Right now, Jan," Rowan said through her own tears. "I'm on my way right now! I'll explain it all when I get there, which should be about two more hours."

She hung up before Jan could shoot any more questions at her. She wanted to get on the road again, back to Ten Oaks. Back to Neal!

Jan greeted her with a smothering hug. "You won't be sorry, Row. I know it!" She smiled at Rowan through happy tears. "This is an answer to prayer," she said fervently.

"I know, Jan." Rowan sniffed happily. "And, Jan, I'm sorry about some of the things I said—and thought—about your prayers."

"Don't be, Row. You still had your grief to work

through and anyway, everything has worked out for the best." She looked at Rowan fondly.

"Do you love him, Row?" Jan asked softly.

Rowan gave a puzzled little laugh. "That's the funny thing, Jan. I honestly don't know. It's all too new, I guess. But I do know I care a great deal, enough that I couldn't wait to see him again."

Jan's expressive eyes clouded as she looked at Rowan's glowing face. "But Neal isn't here right now, Row."

"He isn't here?" She winced at the painful spasm that squeezed her insides. "Did he know I was coming?" she whispered.

"Yes, I told him, but there was an emergency at the Austin plant. In fact, the manager there called practically as soon as you hung up. Row, don't look like that," Jan pleaded. "He'll be back. He *had* to go."

Was the "emergency" that had called him away been her coming back? Otherwise, wouldn't he have left some message for her?

"Did he say anything before he left, Jan?"

"No. No, I'm sorry, he didn't, Rowan. But, really, he left in such a hurry, I'm sure he'll call as soon as he can."

But he didn't call, not once as the incredibly long days crept by. Rowan scarcely ventured from the house, afraid of missing his call. Her emotions swung madly from hope he would call any minute, to being absolutely sure that he deliberately wasn't calling because he knew she was there.

She was emotionally exhausted and the euphoric high of her impulsive decision to come back had evaporated to mere tenacity. Now she was determined to stay and see if he really would put in an appearance while she was here.

Despite Jan's optimism, she knew in her heart she had made a mistake in coming back. She felt that she teetered on the brink of an abyss, but couldn't pull back. She couldn't stay indefinitely, waiting, but she couldn't make herself leave, either.

The thought of leaving the hills made her stomach queasy and her hands ice-cold. The road here had been so painful, it was almost more than she could bear. In despair, she wandered outside, absorbing the sights and sounds she had come to love.

The rat-a-tat of a woodpecker broke the silence and she tilted her head back to see his red crest against the green foliage high in one of the ancient oaks.

She noticed that the storm-damaged trees had leafed out nicely, the shiny dark green leaves effectively camouflaging the scars. In fact, hardly a vestige of the devastating tornado was visible as her steps led her toward the stable to see Toby.

Red-caned blackberry brambles snatched at her jeans as she ambled down the path, the prickly stems heavy with the green nubbins that would be succulent berries before long. Yellow-green bittersweet vines snaked up the tree trunks at the edge of the woods, laden with the clusters of pods that would burst open at first frost to reveal autumn-orange berries. How she longed to be here then!

Her eyes adjusted quickly to the dimness of the stable and her nose wrinkled at the unfamiliar but not unpleasant odor of hay and horses. At least Slim didn't seem to be disturbed by her presence. She had encountered him here the day before, to her dismay, but he greeted her with a polite nod, as always. But Slim was so tight-lipped, who could guess his feelings?

She dawdled through the central corridor toward Toby's enclosure, passing through bars of late afternoon sunlight that searched through the high windows. Lacy cobwebs festooned the stalls and dancing dust motes performed as she moved.

The memory of her last encounter here with Neal still haunted her. A brief flicker of apprehension caused her pulse to beat erratically and she quickened her pace toward the open doors.

Toby nickered softly at her approach and she relaxed as he nuzzled unerringly at the sugar cubes in her jeans pocket. "Here you are, boy." She rubbed the rough head. "One at a time, Toby boy, don't be greedy."

A sudden alertness in the animal caught her attention and a chill snaked up her spine as she reluctantly looked over her shoulder.

She turned around in slow motion and jammed her icy hands into her pockets to still their trembling. She had to swallow hard before speaking.

"I came back," she said inanely.

"So I see," Neal said flatly. He stood rooted to the spot, his tall form casting a long shadow, the sun behind him creating a nimbus on the white mane.

Her heart skipped a beat with a dizzying sense of expectation and in that instant she knew intuitively that she must take the initiative. She moved hesitantly through the sunlight and shadows toward him, her eyes never leaving his face.

He watched her guardedly, his gray eyes frosty, chilling her even in the heat of the stable.

She breathed a little prayer as each step carried her closer and closer to him. Finally she stood before him and raised thickly fringed green eyes to meet his own steady stare.

He drew in a ragged breath as he read the peace and knowledge in the crystal green mirrors of her soul, a message that caused the muscles to quiver in the brawny arms that reached for her.

She looked down at the brown strength of the hands extended her, each dark hair standing out crisply and separately. Her own small hands lifted and she clasped his work-roughened fingers.

They stood at arm's length, their hands a bridge between them that neither knew how to cross. Of their own volition, her fingers began a soft exploration of his calloused hands.

"Why, Rowan?" His hands trembled in her grasp.

She held his hands more firmly, pulling him closer. He moved willingly, looming over her.

"Why did you come back?" he repeated.

"Because I had to tell you you were right." She raised shining eyes to look at him with wonder. "I finally realized that life does go on. And, Neal, I know now that God didn't desert me," she admitted. "It was the other way around and he was waiting for me when I came back," she finished triumphantly.

"I'm happy for you, Rowan," he said gamely. He *was* happy for her, but it wasn't what he wanted to hear. But she had come back to tell him.

"About Slim . . ."

"I know all about your conversation with Slim. Why, he could hardly wait to tell me about your plans to put old Toby back to work. If it had been anyone else, I would have said he was excited about the prospect of teaching a bunch of kids to ride!"

Well, at least that worry was put to rest.

"And, Neal, something else." She didn't know how to tell him how she felt, or rather, that she didn't know how she felt about him.

"Yes?" Something leaped in his chest as her fingers tightened on his.

"What you said." She stopped as she felt the blood rush to her hairline. "You know, in my apartment, the other night?"

"You mean when I apologized?" Suddenly he wanted to shout with joy, but only his mouth twitched in a suppressed smile, half-hidden by the shadowing mustache.

"No." Her voice was faint as she looked down at their intertwined fingers. "No, after that."

"After that? Hmmm, let's see." He pretended to search his memory, watching her through half-closed lids. "Oh, you must mean when I said I knew we could never get together."

"No," she mumbled and pulled her hands away.

His arm reached out and one calloused finger lifted her chin, forcing her to look up at him. "Oh, then you must mean when I said 'I love you'," he said softly.

She lifted her chin higher and her eyes sparkled with mischief. "Was *that* what it was! I knew you had said something else!"

Somehow she was in his arms, folded close against his chest. "Yes, that's what it was, you little minx." He hugged her hard against him, his face buried in her hair. "Now, what about it?"

When she didn't answer, he held her away from him, his strong hands gripping both arms. "What about it, Rowan?" he demanded.

She looked up at him, her heart in her eyes as she studied every ruggedly handsome feature of his face for an endless moment.

His hands tightened on her arms and the muscle tensed in his jaw. "What is it, Rowan? Is there something you wanted to tell me?"

Her soft lips curved in an enchanting smile. "Just this, Neal." Her face was radiant as she reached out to cup his face in ringless fingers. "After you left, I realized I cared for you, too. Very deeply." A slim finger stilled his lips as he started to speak. "I honestly don't know at this point if I love you the way you want me to. But, Neal, I can feel again! I care, deep inside!"

"Come here," he whispered huskily. Twin points of fire glowed in the gray depths of his eyes as he pulled her back against him.

As she went willingly into his arms and her lips met his, she could feel the last of the icy block around her heart melt and rivers of warmth flood through her whole being.

Her fingers caressed the muscular column of his throat to wander to the coarse hair in the nape of his neck, where they buried themselves in the white mane, pulling him closer.

His arms enveloped her as if to never let her go. His lips were sealed to hers until she was breathless with his insistent kisses. She gave herself up to his eager lips, her own moist mouth accepting his claim.

He lifted his head and she drew back ever so little.

"Neal?" She raised troubled eyes to look at him. "There's one other thing," she cautioned.

"What, little one?" He kept one arm firmly around her and reached up to her hair with the other to caressingly brush away a straw that had sifted down from the hayloft.

"There's no way I can ever completely forget them, you know," she whispered.

"I know, my darling." He folded her against him again. "And I wouldn't want you to." She could feel his lips move against her hair. "That's all part of what makes you such a wonderful, loving woman."

"I'm not at all sure I'm wonderful, Neal, but I'm sure—now—that I can again be loving."

His lips made little forays over her eyelids, down her flushed cheeks, back to her mouth. "Let me help you make up your mind, little one."

"Somehow, I don't think that's going to be difficult at all."

ABOUT THE AUTHOR

GEORGIA DALLAS is director of a public library in Illinois. She has written a book review column and press releases for local newspapers. This is her first novel. Dallas and her husband have three grown children.

A Letter to Our Readers

Dear Reader:

Welcome to Serenade Books—a series designed to bring you beautiful love stories in the world of inspirational romance. They will uplift you, encourage you, and provide hours of wholesome entertainment, so thousands of readers have testified. That we might better contribute to your reading enjoyment, we would appreciate your taking a few minutes to respond to the following questions and return to:

> Lois Taylor
> Serenade Books
> The Zondervan Publishing House
> 1415 Lake Drive, S.E.
> Grand Rapids, Michigan 49506

1. Did you enjoy reading *This Band of Gold?*
    - ☐ Very much. I would like to see more books by this author!
    - ☐ Moderately
    - ☐ I would have enjoyed it more if _____

2. Where did you purchase this book? _____

3. What influenced your decision to purchase this book?
    - ☐ Cover
    - ☐ Title
    - ☐ Publicity
    - ☐ Back cover copy
    - ☐ Friends
    - ☐ Other _____

4. Please rate the following elements from 1 (poor) to 10 (superior).
   - ☐ Heroine
   - ☐ Hero
   - ☐ Setting
   - ☐ Plot
   - ☐ Inspirational theme
   - ☐ Secondary characters

5. What are some inspirational themes you would like to see treated in future books?
   _____
   _____

6. Please indicate your age range:
   - ☐ Under 18
   - ☐ 18–24
   - ☐ 25–34
   - ☐ 35–45
   - ☐ 46–55
   - ☐ Over 55

Serenade/Saga books are inspirational romances in historical settings, designed to bring you a joyful, heart-lifting reading experience.

Serenade/Saga books available in your local bookstore:

#1 *Summer Snow,* Sandy Dengler
#2 *Call Her Blessed,* Jeanette Gilge
#3 *Ina,* Karen Baker Kletzing
#4 *Juliana of Clover Hill,* Brenda Knight Graham
#5 *Song of the Nereids,* Sandy Dengler
#6 *Anna's Rocking Chair,* Elaine Watson
#7 *In Love's Own Time,* Susan C. Feldhake
#8 *Yankee Bride,* Jane Peart
#9 *Light of My Heart,* Kathleen Karr
#10 *Love Beyond Surrender,* Susan C. Feldhake
#11 *All the Days After Sunday,* Jeanette Gilge
#12 *Winterspring,* Sandy Dengler
#13 *Hand Me Down the Dawn,* Mary Harwell Sayler
#14 *Rebel Bride,* Jane Peart
#15 *Speak Softly, Love,* Kathleen Yapp
#16 *From This Day Forward,* Kathleen Karr
#17 *The River Between,* Jacquelyn Cook
#18 *Valiant Bride,* Jane Peart
#19 *Wait for the Sun,* Maryn Langer
#20 *Kincaid of Cripple Creek,* Peggy Darty
#21 *Love's Gentle Journey,* Kay Cornelius
#22 *Applegate Landing,* Jean Conrad
#23 *Beyond the Smoky Curtain,* Mary Harwell Sayler

#24 *To Dwell in the Land,* Elaine Watson
#25 *Moon for a Candle,* Maryn Langer
#26 *The Conviction of Charlotte Grey,* Jeanne Cheyney
#27 *Opal Fire,* Sandy Dengler
#28 *Divide the Joy,* Maryn Langer
#29 *Cimarron Sunset,* Peggy Darty
#30 *This Rolling Land,* Sandy Dengler
#31 *The Wind Along the River,* Jacquelyn Cook
#32 *Sycamore Settlement,* Suzanne Pierson Ellison
#33 *Where Morning Dawns,* Irene Brand
#34 *Elizabeth of Saginaw Bay,* Donna Winters
#35 *Westward My Love,* Elaine L. Schulte
#36 *Ransomed Bride,* Jane Peart
#37 *Dreams of Gold,* Elaine L. Schulte

Serenade/Saga books are now being published in a new, longer length:

#T1 *Chessie's King,* Kathleen Karr
#T2 *The Rogue's Daughter,* Molly Noble Bull
#T3 *Image in the Looking Glass,* Jacquelyn Cook
#T4 *Rising Thunder,* Carolyn Ann Wharton
#T5 *Fortune's Bride,* Jane Peart
#T6 *Cries the Wilderness Wind,* Susan Kirby
#T7 *Come Gentle Spring,* Irene Brand
#T8 *Seasons of the Heart,* Susan Feldhake
#T9 *Ride with Wings,* Maryn Langer
#T10 *Golden Gates,* Jean Conrad
#T11 *Sycamore Steeple,* Suzanne Pierson Ellison

Serenade / Serenata books are inspirational romances in contemporary settings, designed to bring you a joyful, heart-lifting reading experience.

Serenade / Serenata books available in your local bookstore:

- #1 *On Wings of Love,* Elaine L. Schulte
- #2 *Love's Sweet Promise,* Susan C. Feldhake
- #3 *For Love Alone,* Susan C. Feldhake
- #4 *Love's Late Spring,* Lydia Heermann
- #5 *In Comes Love,* Mab Graff Hoover
- #6 *Fountain of Love,* Velma S. Daniels and Peggy E. King
- #7 *Morning Song,* Linda Herring
- #8 *A Mountain to Stand Strong,* Peggy Darty
- #9 *Love's Perfect Image,* Judy Baer
- #10 *Smoky Mountain Sunrise,* Yvonne Lehman
- #11 *Greengold Autumn,* Donna Fletcher Crow
- #12 *Irresistible Love,* Elaine Anne McAvoy
- #13 *Eternal Flame,* Lurlene McDaniel
- #14 *Windsong,* Linda Herring
- #15 *Forever Eden,* Barbara Bennett
- #16 *Call of the Dove,* Madge Harrah
- #17 *The Desires of Your Heart,* Donna Fletcher Crow
- #18 *Tender Adversary,* Judy Baer
- #19 *Halfway to Heaven,* Nancy Johanson
- #20 *Hold Fast the Dream,* Lurlene McDaniel
- #21 *The Disguise of Love,* Mary LaPietra
- #22 *Through a Glass Darkly,* Sara Mitchell
- #23 *More Than a Summer's Love,* Yvonne Lehman

#24 *Language of the Heart,* Jeanne Anders
#25 *One More River,* Suzanne Pierson Ellison
#26 *Journey Toward Tomorrow,* Karyn Carr
#27 *Flower of the Sea,* Amanda Clark
#28 *Shadows Along the Ice,* Judy Baer
#29 *Born to Be One,* Cathie LeNoir
#30 *Heart Aflame,* Susan Kirby
#31 *By Love Restored,* Nancy Johanson
#32 *Karaleen,* Mary Carpenter Reid
#33 *Love's Full Circle,* Lurlene McDaniel
#34 *A New Love,* Mab Graff Hoover
#35 *The Lessons of Love,* Susan Phillips
#36 *For Always,* Molly Noble Bull
#37 *A Song in the Night,* Sara Mitchell
#38 *Love Unmerited,* Donna Fletcher Crow
#39 *Thetis Island,* Brenda Willoughby
#40 *Love More Precious,* Marilyn Austin

Serenade/Serenata books are now being published in a new, longer length:

#T1 *Echoes of Love,* Elaine L. Schulte
#T2 *With All Your Heart,* Sara Mitchell
#T3 *Moonglow,* Judy Baer
#T4 *Gift of Love,* Lurlene McDaniel
#T5 *The Wings of Adrian,* Jan Seabaugh
#T6 *Song of Joy,* Elaine L. Schulte
#T7 *Island Dawn,* Annetta Hutton
#T8 *Heartstorm,* Carol Blake Gerrond
#T9 *After the Storm,* Margaret Johnson
#T10 *Through the Valley of Love,* Shirley Cook